"I should have told you," Chance's brother admitted to him.

"And her. Did you see the look on Andi's face when she first saw me? She doesn't want me on this trip. Is this some plot to create family harmony between Andi and me?"

Bowie glanced at him. "Something like that."

Chance didn't trust the gleam in Bowie's eyes. "Oh, no, you don't."

"Just get to know her. You two got off to a rocky start, but—"

"Are you insane? I can't believe you're seriously trying to fix me up with…with her! This is a terrible idea."

Bowie set his jaw. "Is it? I saw the way you looked at her when she climbed out of the fountain, like somebody hit you between the eyes with a two-by-four."

Chance kept his voice low, despite his rising blood pressure. "Which is about what I expected to happen next! Whenever she's around it's like being in a disaster movie. Coming this summer to theaters near you—*Andi.*"

Dear Reader,

Going Overboard. Sandra and the Scoundrel. I think the titles of this month's LOVE & LAUGHTER books explain themselves and the appeal of romantic comedy. After all, what's better than experiencing opposites finding romance and humor!

Spectacular Vicki Lewis Thompson continues her winning stories with *Going Overboard,* otherwise known as the houseboat cruise from hell. Ever the adventurer, Vicki undertook her own houseboat trip and, as a result, has firsthand experience of many of the mishaps found in the novel. Since then, Vicki's become a real land lover.

Always funny Jacqueline Diamond pens her second LOVE & LAUGHTER romance about a secondary character from *Punchline.* Sandra Duval is everything a flighty heiress should be (including owning and wearing an outrageous collection of bizarre hats and costumes) and completely lovable as she is confronted with the complete unknown: children!

So, have a laugh on us and enjoy the romance!

Malle Vallik

Malle Vallik
Associate Senior Editor

GOING OVERBOARD
Vicki Lewis Thompson

Harlequin Books

TORONTO • NEW YORK • LONDON
AMSTERDAM • PARIS • SYDNEY • HAMBURG
STOCKHOLM • ATHENS • TOKYO • MILAN
MADRID • WARSAW • BUDAPEST • AUCKLAND

ISBN 0-373-44031-6

GOING OVERBOARD

Copyright © 1997 by Vicki Lewis Thompson

A funny thing happened...

As research for this book, three inexperienced friends and I spent some time on a houseboat not too long ago. It wasn't pretty. I was the genius who suggested renting the biggest houseboat on the lake. After all, bigger is better, isn't it? I had visions of Cleopatra's barge—the reality was closer to the *Titanic*. The four of us survived the trip, but as for the boat, let's just say it was fortunate we decided to take out propeller insurance.

—Vicki Lewis Thompson

Books by Vicki Lewis Thompson

HARLEQUIN LOVE & LAUGHTER
  5—STUCK WITH YOU
 17—ONE MOM TOO MANY

HARLEQUIN TEMPTATION
555—THE TRAILBLAZER
559—THE DRIFTER
563—THE LAWMAN
600—HOLDING OUT FOR A HERO
624—MR. VALENTINE
642—THE HEARTBREAKER

Don't miss any of our special offers. Write to us at the following address for information on our newest releases.

Harlequin Reader Service
U.S.: 3010 Walden Ave., P.O. Box 1325, Buffalo, NY 14269
Canadian: P.O. Box 609, Fort Erie, Ont. L2A 5X3

To my three shipmates on the Houseboat from Hell.
As long as you're prompt with your checks,
your identities will remain our little secret.

1

_____

"I'M WORRIED ABOUT how the stripper will go over."
Andi Lombard expertly popped the cork from the champagne bottle and poured the bubbly into the crystal punch
bowl being refilled at her elbow. "With the exception of
my little sis, Nicole, those women in your living room
seem kind of..."

"Repressed?" Ginger Thorson grinned as she added
the punch mix.

"No kidding! All the nightgowns Nicole has opened so
far must've come from the Vestal Virgin Boutique."

"I'll bet the one you bought isn't like that."

Andi winked. "No, ma'am. Nicole will have to hose
Bowie down after she models it for him." She put the
empty champagne bottle on the counter. "We need to do
something, Ging. How many more of these bottles do you
have?"

"That's the last one I have chilled, but there's more in
the cupboard. I just thought—"

"Chill 'em. And let's bring out the salty snacks to get
them thirsty. If these uptight matrons don't start slugging
back the champagne punch, my stripper is going to
bomb."

"You want to get them smashed?"

"The way I see it, I'm removing their inhibitions so
they'll get the most out of the experience."

"Including your sister's future mother-in-law?"

"That woman is a pain, Ginger. Did you notice how she acted when we met?"

"A little snobbish, I'll admit."

"A little?" Andi drew herself up, adjusted an imaginary set of glasses and stared disapprovingly down her nose as Ginger began to giggle. "Good evening, my dear," Andi mimicked. "You must be Andi. Nicole tells me you live in *Las Vegas*." Andi looked as if she'd smelled something bad as she pronounced the name of the city. "But then, I suppose everyone has to live *somewhere*."

"You're right. She is a pain," Ginger said, laughing.

"Admit it, you'd like to see her ripped."

"I would." Ginger opened a cupboard and pulled out chips and pretzels. "Forget the petits fours. We'll serve these." She dumped the snacks into bowls and took a handful of chips. "I like this stuff better, anyway. You can be on punch patrol."

"And let's take a break from opening presents and get some games going. Do you have Pin the Penis On the Man?"

Ginger nearly choked on her mouthful of chips.

"I guess you don't," Andi said, patting her friend on the back. She dipped a cup in the punch and handed it to her. "Sorry about that."

Ginger took a gulp of the punch and cleared her throat. "Andi, these women would pass out if they heard the word *penis* spoken aloud."

"Okay, then how about Twister? That's fun."

"They expect sedate paper-and-pencil games."

Andi groaned.

"As long as they're sitting down, they'll be able to drink more," Ginger told her.

"Then let's get to it. I'm afraid pouring punch down them is the only way we're gonna save this evening."

"Andi Lombard, you are a wicked, wicked lady." Ginger picked up the punch bowl. "And thank God you showed up."

She wouldn't have dreamed of *not* showing up, Andi thought as she followed Ginger into the living room with the chips and pretzels. After all, her baby sister was getting married, and they'd always been there for each other. As globe-trotting military brats, they'd faced new base housing, new schools and new playmates with a united front. Andi had shared with her sister the friends she made so easily, and Nicole had kept Andi from flunking out.

Then Andi had watched with pride and a touch of envy as little Nicole graduated from college and landed an accounting job at prestigious Jefferson Sporting Goods of Chicago. Meanwhile, Andi had decided to abandon her search for the perfect major at the University of Nevada, and in the past few years had turned her hand to everything from dealing blackjack to selling jet-skis. Nothing held her interest for long.

In two days Nicole would marry Bowie Jefferson, younger brother of Chauncey M. Jefferson the Fourth, the man who ran the sporting goods company. Andi hadn't met this latest in the line of Roman-numeral Chaunceys, a guy who liked to be called *Chance*. Nicole had told her that he was cute, but strictly a type A who thought only about business. Bowie, thank the Lord, was a barrel of laughs. And although Andi was thrilled for her sister, she couldn't quiet the nagging voice telling her that Nicole was making a life, while she—Andi—was making a mess.

She walked into the living room toward her sister and picked up Nicole's camera from an end table, although there had been precious few Kodak moments at this shower. If it weren't for her faith in Bowie to make Nicole's life interesting, she'd kidnap her sister and haul her fanny out of here before she became as boring as this crowd.

A glance at Nicole's punch cup told her the guest of honor hadn't taken time to taste any of the first batch. She leaned toward her sister. "Drink up. Wine is about to flow in torrents around here."

Laughter twinkled in Nicole's clear blue eyes. "And what plot have you and Ginger been hatching in the kitchen, as if I couldn't guess?"

"Trust me, your shower will become much more interesting if you're three sheets to the wind," Andi said under her breath. Then she turned to the assembled women. "Anyone for charades?"

Nicole's muffled laugh was the only thing filling the silence as all the women stared at Andi.

Ginger quickly put down the punch bowl and picked up a stack of small notepads from a lamp table. "There's a new guessing game I thought would be fun."

"Guessing games!" Andi smiled. "I have a great idea. Everyone can guess the size of Bowie's pe—um, schlong."

Eyes widened, and a few titters circled the room.

Mrs. Chauncey M. Jefferson the Third, ensconced in a corner wing chair like a monarch on a throne, got red in the face. "I don't think we're going to—"

"We'll all guess the number of children Nicole's going to have," Ginger said quickly. "Then once we've guessed, we shuffle a deck of cards..."

Andi zoned out on the explanation of the dweeby game. Maybe she'd have to kidnap Nicole, after all, along with Bowie, and take them out to Nevada, where they could let loose and have a good time. The tentacles of the Jefferson Sporting Goods money and prestige just might choke the life out of them here in the suburbs of Chicago.

As everyone else played the games Ginger orchestrated, Andi made the rounds, quietly refilling punch cups. She emptied and refilled the punch bowl twice. Nicole still didn't seem to be drinking the punch, but Andi wasn't worried about her sister. In the right atmosphere, Nicole could party with the best of them, even stone-cold sober. Andi liked what she saw happening to the group, however, as laughter grew raucous and postures became more uninhibited.

Then Ginger glanced at her watch and suggested they open the last few gifts. Figuring the punch had done its work, Andi returned to her station beside Nicole and handed her another package wrapped in tasteful white paper with a virginal white bow.

Nicole held up a flannel granny gown and exclaimed over how warm it would keep her.

"Wozy and carm," said a women in a conservative brown suit. "Whoops, I mean *warmy and coze.*" She giggled. "Goodness, what *do* I mean?"

Andi glanced up at Ginger, who was pressing her lips together in what seemed like a desperate attempt not to laugh.

"You're trying to say *warm and cozy,* Edna," said Mrs. Chauncey M. Jefferson the Third. "You shimply got your tongue twishted around your eyeteeth."

"Dolores Jefferson, you sound a little tipsy!" exclaimed a woman sitting demurely on a love seat. Then she began slipping down into the cushions. "And so do I. What fun! I haven't been tipsy in years."

"Nonshense," said Mrs. Chauncey M. "Nobody's tipshy around here. Sit up straight, Mary."

As Mary tried unsuccessfully to right herself on the

love seat, Nicole gripped Andi's shoulder. "Andi, I think they're all—"

"Time for my gift!" Andi said, grabbing the black box decorated with a large red ribbon.

"It's time for coffee," Nicole muttered.

"First open this." Andi plopped the box into Nicole's lap.

"What naughty wrapping!" said a woman whose up-swept hairdo seemed to be coming unraveled. "Naughty, naughty, naughty." She started laughing, as if she'd made a wonderful joke.

"Here goes nothing." Nicole tucked a blond curl behind her ear and lifted the lid of the box as if afraid something might jump out. "Oh...my...God." She slammed down the lid.

"Let us see," said Mrs. Chauncey M. with a wave of her punch cup. "You think we were born yeshterday?"

"Show us," called out another woman.

"Show us," chorused two others, and soon a chant had begun, complete with clapping. *Show us, show us, show us.*

Ginger sat on the floor next to Andi and elbowed her in the ribs. "How's this?"

"Perfectamundo." Andi grinned as she surveyed the results of her handiwork. "The ladies are tight as ticks." She leaned over toward Ginger. "And our little stripper is due any minute." Then she aimed the camera as Nicole slowly opened the box and held up a crotchless black teddy.

Ginger whooped her approval. "You go, girl!"

"I have *always* wanted to see one of those," said Mrs. Chauncey M. "Pass it over, Nicole, deary."

"Me, first," cried Mary, trying to struggle up from the love seat. "You always get to be first, Dolores, *deary*."

"I want to see it, too," said Edna of the brown suit.

As Andi clicked the camera, the women staggered to their feet and clumped together in a laughing, joking circle around Mrs. Chauncey M., who had lunged forward and snatched the sexy lingerie before Mary could get it.

Nicole shook her head slowly. "Unbelievable. My sister comes to town, and within hours my very proper mother-in-law-to-be is examining a crotchless teddy, slurring her speech and calling me *deary*."

Andi lowered the camera. "Enjoy it, Nic. Life just doesn't get much better than this."

"But it will, right?" Ginger nudged her and tipped her head toward the door.

"Let's hope so." Andi glanced at her watch. "It's getting kinda late. I—"

The doorbell rang, and she shot to her feet, the camera in her hand. "Bingo."

"Andi," her sister called after her. "My heart can't take much more. What are you up to now?"

Andi twirled back to her. "The usual. Try some of that punch, sis!" Excitement pumped through her veins as she hurried to the foyer and squinted through the peephole at the visitor on the other side of the door.

Sure enough, a gorgeous specimen stood in the apartment hallway. He'd assumed the guise of a quintessential businessman—beneath an unbuttoned wool topcoat, he wore a navy pinstriped suit and a pale blue dress shirt. He was probably wearing burgundy wingtips that would pass her military father's spit-shine test with flying colors.

As he stood waiting for her to answer the door, he lightly mussed his dark, close-cropped hair, unfastened the top button of his shirt and loosened his red and navy power tie. She would have enjoyed performing those little tasks for him. Even if the women in the room behind her didn't have a good time with this hunk, she would.

His deliciously square-cut jaw had just a hint of five-o'clock shadow, making him look exactly like an executive who'd just spent a long day at the office. He held a briefcase that probably contained a compact sound system. If he performed as beautifully as he'd presented himself, he'd earn a big tip.

Andi unlatched the door.

CHANCE JEFFERSON hated to interrupt Nicole's bridal shower, but he needed her signature on an insurance policy and she kept forgetting to come by his office and take care of it. Once her parents arrived from Germany tomorrow, she'd be completely occupied until the wedding, and he thought it would be worse dealing with insurance policies at the wedding reception. He wasn't letting his new sister-in-law leave on her honeymoon without being properly insured.

God, he was tired. Sighing, he unbuttoned his collar and loosened his tie. Although pleased his brother had found Nicole, Chance felt the heaviness of yet another weight settling on his shoulders. Bowie would never think of things like life insurance, so once again Chance had to remember what responsibilities his father would have assumed had he been alive. Those responsibilities seemed to come thick and fast these days. Bowie's new wife, wonderful as she was, would contribute another one.

A tall blonde in a miniskirt opened the door and gave him an enthusiastic smile. Some of his fatigue evaporated. He took note of spectacular legs and a tight black sweater that stirred his hormonal urges. Her hair was about the same shade as Nicole's, although she wore it longer and more flyaway than Nicole, and there was a similarity to the eyes, although this woman's were hazel, not blue like

Nicole's. At the moment those hazel eyes were full of mischief.

Chance didn't feel in much of a party mood, but he summoned up a smile and held out his hand. "You must be Andi."

"Yes, and you're late!" She took his hand and pulled him through the doorway.

Caught off guard, he allowed himself to be yanked inside. "I wasn't—"

"Never mind giving me excuses. We're wasting time. Let me have your briefcase." She grabbed it out of his hand.

He grabbed it back. "I'll handle this, if you don't mind."

She took hold of the handle again. "You can't do everything! I'll take care of this part. I know how these things work."

"Really?" Fascinated, he let her have the briefcase. He couldn't believe she was planning to handle Nicole's insurance needs, especially after Nicole had described her sister as a lovable, impractical nut.

"Any idiot can operate a tape player. Let's get your coat off." She started working him out of his coat, brushing her body against him in the process, filling his senses with her heady perfume.

"What tape player?" He wondered if he was so tired he was hallucinating.

She paused with the coat half removed. "You don't have one?"

"Well, sure, but not—"

She abandoned her task, leaving his coat dangling from one arm, and came around to stand in front of him, hands on hips. "Look, you're not on anything, are you?"

He took his coat the rest of the way off and tossed it

on the hall table. "I don't know what you're talking about."

"The hell you don't. Let's take a look." In another totally unexpected move, she put both hands on his shoulders and pulled him forward to peer into his eyes.

He caught his breath, too entranced by this close-up view to protest. Looking into those hazel eyes of hers, he could think of nothing but what it would be like to kiss her. He couldn't understand it. He'd been sane before she opened the door, but now he wouldn't testify to having any brain cells working.

"Your pupils don't look dilated, but I swear, if you've come here doped up, I'll report you."

He gazed down at her and detected a flicker of sensual awareness in her eyes. "Who're you going to tell?" he asked softly.

She released him just as quickly as she'd grabbed him and pushed him toward the living room. "Never mind who I'll tell. Just get in there."

He stood his ground. No matter how sexy she was, he wouldn't be ordered around. "I'll need my briefcase."

"I told you that I'd take care of that part."

"I don't think so." He made a grab for the briefcase, but she jerked it out of reach.

"I'll do it! Will you *please* get into that room and start stripping before those women sober up?"

He stared at her, unable to process the whole sentence at once. First he had to digest the part about her wanting him to strip in front of a group of women including his mother. He had just about worked his way around that and was heading for the *sober up* part, when the doorbell rang.

She grimaced. "Oh, for heaven's sake. Wait a second. I don't want you starting without me."

"Not on your life."

She strode back to the door and jerked it open.

A guy in a police uniform stood there, grinning at her. "Somebody called about a loud party up here."

"Sorry, Officer, we'll keep it down," Andi said, and started to close the door.

He stuck out his hand and held the door open. "Just a second. You'd better get me Andi Lombard."

She opened the door wider. "I'm Andi."

"Hello, Andi. I'm your stripper."

Chance folded his arms and waited. He told himself not to feel the least bit sorry for her. She'd hired a stripper for a party that included wives of major stockholders. That included his *mother,* for God's sake. She'd also apparently gotten them all blotto. She deserved this little moment.

He felt sorry for her, anyway.

She stood motionless, her back to him. Finally she spoke, her voice high and squeaky. "Would you both excuse me for a minute?" Then she walked out the door, past the confused stripper.

Chance followed her out the door. "Stay right there. Don't do anything," he said to the man.

"I'm paid by the job, not the hour. I can wait."

He found her several feet down the apartment hall, her face the color of a stoplight, her eyes squeezed shut as she pumped her fists up and down in an obvious effort not to scream.

"Andi, listen, I—"

She went immediately still but kept her eyes shut. "A kind person would just shoot me."

God, she was cute with her color high like that. Too cute for his own good. "I'll leave the papers for Nicole on the hall table," he said. "Have her sign where I indicated and get them back to me tomorrow."

She nodded, still not opening her eyes.

He started to say something else, something to ease her embarrassment, but thought better of it. His position didn't allow him to condone this kind of behavior, even if the perpetrator was the most adorable screwup he'd met in years.

He walked back to the apartment, took the papers out of his briefcase and left them where she'd see them. Then he picked up his topcoat and walked out. As he passed the stripper still standing outside the doorway, he paused. "Just remember that most of the women in that room have only seen one naked man in their lives. Go easy on them."

2

SEVEN LONG MONTHS since she'd seen Nicole, Andi thought as she paced the gate area of the Las Vegas airport, waiting for her sister and Bowie to walk through the jetway. This houseboat trip on Lake Mead, just the three of them, was a great idea, and she had Nicole to thank for it. For one thing, she'd get to see Nicole before the baby was born in two months, and for the other, Nicole would be able to give her some guidance as she struggled, at long last, to get some direction in her life.

The prospect of becoming an aunt had trained a spotlight on her own unsettled lifestyle and made her yearn for more stability. Maybe she'd found something worth pursuing in her latest venture of teaching yoga, but she wasn't quite sure, and desperately wanted some validation from Nicole. It was, she thought with a smile, sort of like running to Nicole with her unfinished term paper, the way she'd done so many times when they were younger. Nicole would know what to do.

Andi had been having similar thoughts for quite a while, even before the wedding, but that hadn't been a time for long talks with Nicole. After the disaster with Chance Jefferson at the bridal shower, Andi had tried to keep a low profile. In fact, she'd specifically been trying to avoid him when she'd toppled over backward into the hotel fountain during the reception. She was certain he thought she'd had too much to drink, when actually she'd stayed away from the trays of champagne flutes. She didn't want to get tipsy and embarrass herself.

And it *really* wasn't her fault that two of those waiters had been so busy watching her climb out of the fountain they'd run into each other. Could she help it if Chance had been right in the line of fire when the champagne trays went flying? Thank God she wouldn't have to spend much time in Chance's company. Between being attracted to his good looks and intimidated by his efficiency, she became a basket case every time he showed up.

She concentrated on the flow of people from the black tunnel of the jetway, and finally spied Nicole. With a shriek of welcome, she hurried forward, arms outstretched. "Come here, you pudgy woman!"

"I am not pudgy!" Nicole hugged her fiercely. "I'm just smuggling a small watermelon."

"You look darling carrying a watermelon."

"Doesn't she?" Bowie came up behind her, holding a duffel bag. His good-natured face beneath a thatch of sandy hair had filled out a little, probably due to Nicole's cooking, Andi figured.

Andi released her sister and turned to give him a hug. "Hey, what do you mean, knocking up my sister?"

"It's what guys do," he said. "I can see we need to have a talk about the facts of life. How've you been? Fallen in any fountains lately?"

Andi pulled his head down and whispered in his ear, "That's a dangerous thing to say when we'll be on a houseboat together for a week. Accidents happen, you know."

"Andi," Nicole said, a tremulous quality to her voice, "we have the best surprise."

Andi turned toward her sister. "Twins?"

"No." She glanced behind her.

For the first time, Andi's field of vision lengthened to take in more than her sister and brother-in-law, and when she saw who was standing behind them, suited up as if for Michigan Avenue, briefcase in hand, she gulped.

"Look who agreed to come on the trip," Nicole said. "The four of us will have a ball, don't you think?"

As Andi looked into Chance Jefferson's blue eyes, she saw her own astonishment mirrored there.

He glanced at Bowie. "Andi's going, too?"

HE'D BEEN SET UP. And so had Andi, judging from the look on her face when she'd first seen him. As they headed toward baggage claim, Andi and Nicole walked ahead, lost in conversation. Chance hoped it was about bassinets and crib mobiles; he feared it was about him. Andi had her arm around her sister. At first, Chance had wondered if she'd back out, knowing he was part of the package, but apparently she was willing to suffer through a week in his company to be with Nicole.

Chance grabbed Bowie's arm and dropped back a few paces.

Bowie sighed. "Okay, so I should have told you."

"And *her*. Did you see the look on her face when she first saw me? She doesn't want me on this trip."

"Nicole wanted to tell both of you, but I was afraid at least one of you would cancel if you knew. Nicole and I cut cards to settle the argument about telling or not, and I won."

Chance kept his voice low. "So what's the deal? Is this some plot to create family harmony between Andi and me?"

Bowie glanced at him. "Something like that."

Chance didn't trust the gleam in Bowie's eyes. "Oh, no, you don't."

"Just get to know her, Chance."

"Hey, I'm not interested in—"

"She's a great gal. You two got off to a rocky start, but—"

"Are you insane? I can't believe you're seriously trying to fix me up with your wife's sister. There's, conservatively, a million-to-one chance of it working out, and that leaves a hell of a lot of room for total chaos. This is a terrible idea, Bowie."

Bowie set his jaw. "Is it? I saw the way you looked at her when she climbed out of the fountain, like somebody hit you between the eyes with a two-by-four."

"Which is about what I expected to happen next! Whenever she's around it's like being in a disaster movie. Coming this summer, to theaters near you—*Andi*."

"You looked that way when you went bonkers over Myra Oglethorpe in tenth grade," Bowie persisted.

"You can't possibly remember how I looked at Myra Oglethorpe."

"Wanna bet? I was the kid brother. You were like a god to me. I remember the orchid corsage you bought her for the Christmas dance. I remember the burgundy cummerbund you didn't want to wear until Mom told you it made you look like Tom Selleck. You were so nervous you passed out ten minutes before you were supposed to leave with Dad to pick her up."

Chance's eyes narrowed as he looked at his brother. "And you threatened to tell her all about it at the bus stop on Monday unless I gave you twenty bucks."

Bowie shrugged. "So I was into blackmail. A guy has to supplement his allowance somehow."

"Now I know why I came on this trip. So you could remind me of all those golden memories. Dammit, Bowie, I think I'll snag my luggage and take it back upstairs to the ticket counter. I have a ton of work to do, and Andi would love to see me disappear. I'd save us all a lot of trouble."

"I wish you wouldn't."

"Look, if you're trying to get something started between Andi and me, I might as well leave. I can see it's a mistake, even if you can't."

"It's not just that."

"So what else?"

"This is supposed to be my birthday trip, right? The one Dad always took us on a week or two after our birthdays."

The role he'd been shoved into so abruptly began wrapping its tentacles around him. "Yeah, but—"

"When you said we could take this trip together, I felt like..." Bowie looked away. "Well, like we were keeping something important going."

Hell. Chance knew a killer argument when he heard one. Bowie had instinctively appealed to his sense of tradition and responsibility. As much as he might want to fly back to Chicago, as much as Andi might want him to, he was stuck here.

"Okay, I'll stay," he said quietly. "But this matchmaking thing is not happening, Bowie. I—" He was distracted by the beeping of a cart whisking passengers to a gate. It bore down on Andi and Nicole, their heads together in serious discussion, oblivious to the world around them.

"Nicole! Watch out!" he called, sprinting forward.

Andi looked up first and pushed Nicole out of the way, but the cart had to swerve to avoid Andi. It sideswiped a gift-shop display, which launched glittering souvenir visors and fanny packs out into the terminal. The smooth soles of Chance's dress shoes found a slick spot on the floor and he landed on his butt amid the scattered merchandise. Fortunately, a fanny pack cushioned his briefcase as it slammed to the floor. And so it continues, he thought. *Andi, The Movie.*

ANDI WOULD WALK through hell for her sister, and hell it would be this week, she thought as she drove her van toward Lake Mead. They'd all bought visors and fanny packs from the disrupted gift stand as a peace gesture, and everyone wore a visor except Chance, who'd stuck his in his briefcase. Andi supposed it didn't go with his suit, but he should have put it on just to demonstrate solidarity, in her opinion. Not that he gave a damn about her opinion.

Before the latest incident, Nicole had been explaining that Chance desperately needed a break from his crushing responsibilities and besides that, he and Bowie needed time to bond. She'd been laying the blame on Bowie for not notifying Andi about this little surprise appearance, when the courtesy cart had nearly taken them both out. Andi figured she might as well get used to that sort of pandemonium. It never failed to happen when she was around Chance.

For the moment, she concentrated very hard on her driving, which wasn't simple considering that Chance sat in the passenger seat next to her. It was a logical arrangement, along with assigning Bowie and Nicole to the middle seat. The rest of the van was stuffed with luggage and the gear she'd brought. Bowie had packed an extra sleeping bag for Chance, and brought an extra fishing pole. As long as they caught fish, the groceries Andi had bought would probably stretch to four people. Logistically, Chance's presence wouldn't cause a problem. Emotionally—well, she'd just have to try to ignore him.

Ha. What red-blooded woman would be able to ignore

a man who looked like Chance? Too bad he hadn't turned out to be a stripper. So far today he'd taken off his suit coat and tie after experiencing Las Vegas in the middle of an August heat wave, but that was the extent of his disrobing. A faint scent of expensive men's cologne drifted across to Andi as he shifted in his seat to say a few words to Bowie.

In the midst of the conversation, a phone rang.

Andi glanced around before realizing the noise came from the briefcase at Chance's feet. "Your briefcase is ringing," she said.

"Yeah. Excuse me." He pulled it onto his lap, flipped it open and took out a cellular phone.

While Nicole pointed out landmarks to Bowie, Chance spoke at length with the person on the phone and made notes on a pad he pulled out of a briefcase pocket. He looked as if he were sitting in his office back on Michigan Avenue. If he kept this up, there would be precious little bonding going on, Andi thought.

"Look at that lake, Nic," Bowie said as Andi took the road leading around it toward the marina. "Smooth as glass."

"I've been looking. I'm dying to get into the water and cool off."

"Me, too," Andi said.

"Control yourself," Bowie said. "I know how you like to fling yourself into the first body of water you come to."

"Sometimes it's more fun to fling someone else into the first body of water I come to," Andi retorted. Although Bowie's teasing helped keep her from obsessing about Chance's being around, her brother-in-law was partly to blame for her having to deal with Chance in the first place. She just might push Bowie overboard. She'd push Nicole overboard, too, except she had to think of the baby.

Chance put the phone back in his briefcase and continued to make notes on the pad.

"Who was that?" Bowie asked.

"Eikelhorn." Chance kept writing.

"You know," Bowie said, "I wonder if he's steering us wrong about that ad agency. I've seen a couple of their ads, and they seem pretty pedestrian to me."

"Mmm." Chance's attention remained on his notes.

"There are a couple of other agencies that might be able to do a better job for us, if you'd like me to check them out."

"Eikelhorn has it under control." Chance underlined something and tapped the end of his pen against the paper. It was obvious he wasn't really listening to what Bowie had said.

"Yeah, well, it was just a thought." Bowie sounded disappointed but resigned.

Andi glanced in the rearview mirror just as Nicole put a comforting hand on Bowie's knee. Then she looked over at Chance, who was still engrossed in the notes he was making, apparently unaware that he'd cavalierly sliced and diced his brother's suggestion. Anger boiled in her. Bowie was a great guy, and he sure as hell didn't deserve to be dismissed like that. Chance might be gorgeous. He might be skilled and efficient at business matters. But he didn't know squat about how to treat his brother.

Andi suddenly didn't feel so intimidated by the man. Chance Jefferson wasn't perfect, after all. In fact, he needed to be taught a thing or two. Apparently, Nicole hadn't made any progress in that department, but then, she'd always been shy about such matters. Time for the second team to take the field.

CHANCE MADE SEVERAL calls on his cellular phone before they reached the marina and, in the process, he concluded that concentrating on business this week would help him keep his mind off Andi. She'd met them at the airport in very short shorts, a skinny little neon-green shirt and high-tops. He could tell she enjoyed flamboyance, although she probably considered him immune to it. He wasn't. Bowie was right about his reaction to her. Despite the disasters that swirled around her, he was fascinated. Come to think of it, the emotions she stirred in him weren't so different from the way he'd felt when he'd fallen for Myra Ogle-thorpe.

But he wasn't in tenth grade anymore, even though there were days he wished he were, days when he'd give anything to abandon the prestige and money in favor of freedom. It wasn't an option.

"Well, gang, here we are." Andi parked the van next to the marina. "I'll get the paperwork taken care of if you'll load everything into those wheeled carts down by the dock." Then she hopped out of the van, grabbed a folder of papers and started toward the registration office.

Chance watched the hypnotizing motion of her bottom for about two seconds too long and Bowie caught him at it. "Well, what are we waiting for?" he asked briskly, ignoring Bowie's grin as he stepped into the blast furnace of a Nevada summer day. The growl of outboard motors filled the air and the acrid scent of diesel fuel triggered memories of his uncle's boat and lazy Wisconsin summers. Back then he'd been impatient to grow up, with no clue how precious those carefree days had been.

"Nicole, you just relax your pregnant self," Bowie said. "Chance and I, in an incredibly manly gesture, will load up those carts."

Nicole spread her arms wide. "Ah, vacation."

"Of course, we expect you women to do all the cooking," Bowie added.

Nicole laughed. "I'll be willing to cook whatever you manly men catch, but you'd better not let Andi hear you talking like that. She'll roast you on a spit over the campfire in no time."

Chance didn't doubt that for a minute. In fact, at the wedding reception, prior to the fountain debacle, they'd spent their obligatory dance together as maid of honor and best man arguing about her decision to hire a stripper for Nicole's party. Chance had initiated the argument on purpose once he realized how potently she affected him at close range. She'd obliged his need for conflict by taking the offensive and reminding him that men had hired strippers for bachelor parties for generations. She happened to know, she said, that there had been a stripper at Bowie's party. Chance thought it was the better part of valor not to admit who'd hired her.

"I'll go get us a couple of those carts." Chance headed for the dock, where people dressed in Day-Glo-bright bathing suits or T-shirts and tattered shorts moved leisurely around on rubber thongs. The water looked like heaven, and he had the urge to fling himself into it, suit pants, silk shirt, shoes and all. But that was more of an Andi Lombard thing to do, not a Chance Jefferson move.

He restrained himself and grabbed two carts, which he started pushing toward the van. He also needed to put in a call to Annalise, his secretary, before leaving the marina, to impress upon her that she shouldn't hesitate to call him in an emergency. He wished the Ping Golf representatives hadn't been so irritated when he'd postponed a meeting with them until next week.

He wondered again how his dad had been able to manage the birthday trips that had become such a tradition.

Maybe he'd felt more relaxed because he'd built the business. Chance had the daunting task of keeping it going and making it even better.

He wheeled the carts up to the back of the van, where Bowie stood.

"Brings back memories, doesn't it, bro?" Bowie said with a grin.

"Yeah, it does." He'd only seen Bowie this excited twice in the past year—on his wedding day and when he told Chance about the baby.

Bowie heaved a sleeping bag into one of the carts. "I hope you're not gonna tie yourself to that cell phone the whole week."

"I can't just cut off communication with the office." Chance lifted a full cooler out of the back.

"Dad did."

"Well, I'm not Dad."

Bowie unloaded bags of groceries. "I hope to hell you're not. Dead at fifty-six. That's too young."

"He never got any exercise." Chance put four fishing poles into the cart. By now his shirt was sticking to his back. Damn, but it was hot. "I go to the gym three times a week."

"Even that seems to be a job for you. Be honest, what do you do for fun?"

Chance gave him a smile. "I go on houseboat trips with my brother."

"Ah." Bowie stopped to wipe his sweaty forehead. "So, are we having fun yet?"

"Well, boys, I just signed our life away," Andi said, coming up with the folder of papers, swelled by a few extra documents, in one hand. "We're now the temporary occupants of a ten-person houseboat sitting in slip number ten, A dock."

Chance blinked. "Did you say *ten*-person?"

"Yeah," Bowie put in. "Remember? I told you that the only thing available on short notice was a cancellation from a church party, and they'd rented the biggest boat they had, so we got it."

Chance figured he hadn't been listening carefully when Bowie told him that, because the houseboat plans hadn't been high on his list of priorities. "Just how big is a ten-person boat?" he asked.

Andi thumbed through her papers. "I have the dimensions right here. Aha. Forty-seven by fourteen."

"Feet?" Chance asked.

She looked at him with a deadpan expression. "No, inches. All four of us should fit nicely on a boogie board, don't you think?"

"Hey, so what if it's a big boat?" Bowie said. "More room to party!"

"What's all the commotion about?" Nicole asked, climbing out of the van and coming around to the back.

"Chance seems to think the boat's too big," Andi said.

"No, he doesn't," Bowie said.

"Yes, he does," Chance said.

"Look, as I told Bowie when we made the arrangements," Andi said, "it was the same price as a smaller boat, because they had this last-minute cancellation, and they gave us a special deal. So if you're worried that it's costing us too much money—"

"No, it's not the money. That's just a damn big boat."

"So?" Andi asked.

"So it probably takes more than one motor to run it."

"Well, of course it does," Andi said. "It has—" she paused to consult her papers "—twin screws, according to this. I guess that means two sets of propellers. When I signed up they heckled me about getting propeller insurance, but I said we didn't need that because we had two experienced houseboat pilots in the party.''

"One for each screw," Bowie said with a grin.

Chance scratched the back of his head and looked at Bowie. "Twin screws. Wasn't Uncle Trevor's a single screw?"

"Twin screws, single screw, what difference does it make?" Bowie said. "A houseboat's a houseboat. A motor's a motor. One for you, one for me. Come on, let's get under way."

Andi looked from Chance to Bowie and back to Chance again. "You two are beginning to sound a lot like Laurel and Hardy, and that makes me nervous. You do know what you're doing, right? Neither of you crewed on the *Exxon Valdez* or anything?"

"Very funny," Bowie said.

"'Cause I can always go back and get propeller insurance. They had an example of a pretty ugly shredding job on display, just so you can see what happens if either of you Jacques Cousteaus back that sucker into a pile of rocks."

"I'm sure that won't happen," Nicole said, "considering all the time they spent on their uncle's houseboat."

"Exactly," Bowie said. "Chance and I aren't about to back this baby into the rocks, are we, bro? Propeller insurance. What a joke."

Chance longed for that insurance, but he didn't want to argue with Bowie about it. "We'll do fine. No worries."

Andi gazed at him. "So said the captain of the *Titanic*, I hear."

That finally got his back up. He wasn't used to being questioned. "Trust me, we can handle this. Now, let's stop standing around in the heat, and get aboard our bargain boat."

With Chance pushing one cart and Bowie the other, they started toward the dock. After a brief stop for ice at the general store, where Chance also put in a quick call to Annalise, they continued toward the mooring slip. Andi and Nicole walked ahead of them, showing the way toward slip number ten.

Chance lowered his voice as he leaned toward Bowie. "I take it Uncle Trevor let you run that boat of his?"

"Are you kidding?"

Chance looked at him in alarm. "You didn't ever drive it?"

"Hell, no," Bowie murmured. "Uncle Trev thought I was a complete screwup and wouldn't let me touch the controls, but I figure you have enough experience for both of us."

"And what makes you think I was allowed to operate that boat?"

"Because you were always considered the responsible one, and I—" Bowie brought his cart to an abrupt stop. "Oh my God. He didn't let you, either?"

Chance shook his head.

"Holy Houseboats, Batman. What do we do now?"

"We stay cool." Chance started pushing the cart down the dock and Bowie continued beside him. "We've both seen the ads for these vacations, and nobody mentions having to be experts at boating, right?"

"Right."

"We haven't operated a houseboat, but we've both driven motorboats."

"Yeah," Bowie responded with a little less confidence. "A few times, anyway."

"And there's got to be some sort of manual."

"And we can both read! Hey, I'm liking this plan.

We're smart. Or at least you're smart. We'll figure this out.''

"I just wish we didn't have such a big boat," Chance said.

"Maybe forty-seven by fourteen isn't as big as you think. Maybe—"

Andi spun around to face them and gestured dramatically toward her left. "Here we are! Home sweet home!"

Bowie turned and gulped. "My God, it's an aircraft carrier."

Speechless, Chance stared at the monster tied up to slip number ten. He'd seen ranch homes in the Chicago suburbs smaller than this.

Andi and Nicole seemed as thrilled by the size of the boat as he was dismayed. They swung open the railing gate and hurried aboard, chattering happily about the spacious accommodations.

"It's spacious, all right," Bowie said in a subdued voice. "I'll bet the church group was gonna hold a revival in there."

"Hell, you could take this across the friggin' Atlantic Ocean."

Bowie rubbed the back of his neck. "Here's an idea. We just stay right here. People do that in Seattle, right? Smart people, those Seattlites, living on houseboats that are permanently tied up to the dock. Never worry about sailing anywhere, those folks. We could—"

"Nope. We're going to take this tub out of here, Bowie. Our manhood is at stake."

"Hey, you guys, get a move on," Nicole called from the deck. "If you don't hurry up, Andi's liable to get sick of waiting around and start up those motors herself."

"We're coming!" Chance and Bowie shouted together as they nearly collided in their effort to get aboard.

3

ANDI FELL IN LOVE with all the little nooks and crannies of the houseboat. As she and the others stowed their gear, she kept finding interesting cubbies for stashing stuff. She'd also discovered something else. Chance wasn't as immune to her as she'd imagined. He probably hated the fact that he reacted to her, but react he did. A slight flush and a quicksilver gleam in his blue eyes gave away his X-rated thoughts about her. It could prove useful. She could teach him a lesson about all work and no play— and perhaps teach him to better appreciate his brother.

At last the four of them gathered in the living-room area of the houseboat. Bowie and Nicole's sleeping bags lay in a back double bunk and Chance had chosen a fold-out bed in the living room. Andi would sleep in the middle of the boat on the top bunk of a single set of bunks.

Nicole dusted her hands together. "That's it for the housekeeping chores. Anchors aweigh."

"You bet," Bowie said, grabbing the thick operations manual from the shelf beside the captain's chair.

Chance took the book out of his brother's hands before he'd even opened it. Frowning, he started flipping pages as Bowie peered over his shoulder.

Andi watched the interaction with some impatience, although she had to admit that air of command could be attractive. Chance had rolled up the sleeves of his dress shirt and his arms had a nice flex to the muscle as he turned the pages. A man as disciplined as Chance probably worked out on a regular basis. But how long had it been since he'd thrown a Frisbee or cannonballed into a swimming pool? Probably years.

"So which one of you is taking us out?" she asked.

"He is," they said in unison, pointing to each other.

"Oh, this is good," Andi said, folding her arms.

Bowie gestured toward Chance. "Just deferring to your age and experience, buddy."

Chance sent him a long look before walking into the pilothouse and slowly taking his seat at the controls. "Right." He flexed his shoulders and studied the panel.

"You're both quite sure you can handle this?" Andi asked.

They responded with a flurry of assurances that left her feeling not the least bit reassured.

Chance ran his fingers over the buttons and stood up again. "I'm going aft to take a look at the motors and figure out the best trajectory when we back out."

"Good idea. I'll go with you." As Bowie followed Chance, he said over his shoulder "*Aft* means the rear of the ship."

"Thank you, Captain Ahab," Andi called after him. She turned to Nicole, who was sitting on one of the bench seats. "What do you think, sis? Do they know what they're doing?"

"I'm not sure about Bowie, but I'm under the impression Chance always knows what he's doing."

"He is pretty damn sure of himself. Does it bother you the way he discounts Bowie's contributions?"

"Drives me nuts. But from what I understand, their father treated Bowie the same way. I'm hoping that maybe on this trip…well, we'll see."

"That's assuming we ever get out on the lake."

"Oh, we will," Nicole said. "You and I both know people who've taken houseboat trips with no boating experience at all. These guys at least have some idea of the process, and I'm sure we can manage it. Plus, I *really* need this break, Andi. I didn't realize bearing the first Jefferson heir was going to be such a big deal."

"Is Mrs. Chauncey M. giving you a hard time?"

Nicole gave her a weary smile. "You know those language tapes you're supposed to play while the baby's still in the womb, so the kid is born already programmed to be bilingual?"

"She bought you some of those?"

"No, she hired a French teacher to come over three times a week and talk to my belly."

"No!" Andi started to giggle. "What does Bowie think of this?"

"He doesn't know. It's supposed to be a surprise for him."

"And when is this surprise going to be unveiled? When little whozit sails onto the delivery table shouting *bonjour?*"

Nicole grinned. "I have no idea."

"What does this French person say to your belly?"

"How should I know? I don't speak French."

"Me, neither, but I gotta try this." Still chuckling, she walked over and got down on her knees in front of Nicole. *"Parlez-vous français?"* she murmured, patting Nicole's belly. "Hey, she kicked back! That must mean she understood me!"

"Oh, I'm sure."

Andi searched her memory for French phrases. "Darling, *je vous aime beaucoup.* Let's see—what else? Oh, that little cartoon skunk." She leaned closer to Nicole's belly. *"Pepe le Peu."*

"Oh, do go on," Nicole said, laughing.

"That's all the French I know. No, wait. Food. French food." Between giggles, she leaned forward again. *"Filet mignon,"* she crooned. *"Pâté de foie gras. Croissants.* Come on, Nic. You cook more than I do. Help me communicate with this kid."

Nicole laughed harder. *"Coq au vin."*

"Coq au vin," Andi repeated. She pushed her lips out in a Gallic pout. *"Château...briand. Vichyssoise. Oui, oui, oui,* all zee way home, my little radish."

Nicole laughed until tears ran down her face.

"Will you look at that, Chance?" Bowie said, coming through the hallway. "We leave them for five minutes and all hell breaks loose. What's up, Nic?"

Nicole just shook her head, helpless with laughter.

"It's a surprise," Andi said, getting to her feet. "But I'll give you a hint. Start practicing 'Frère Jacques' in the shower."

Bowie stared at her before turning toward Chance. "You make any sense of this?"

Chance stood gazing at Andi with a bemused expression on his face. He seemed totally absorbed by the playful scene he and Bowie had interrupted, absorbed by Andi, for that matter. Andi looked into his eyes and saw an emotion she hadn't associated with him before—delight. She was encouraged.

"Chance?" Bowie prompted.

Chance snapped out of his reverie and broke eye contact with Andi. "Uh, sorry. What was that?"

"Never mind. You ready to start the motors?" Bowie asked, exchanging a glance with Nicole.

"Yeah, the motors." He walked quickly to the captain's chair and sat down. Then he consulted the control panel a few seconds more before he started flicking switches. Soon the boat hummed and throbbed as the twin engines chugged to life.

Andi watched the mantle of responsibility settle on his shoulders again. Tension tightened his jaw and narrowed his eyes. The boy inside him had been banished, at least for the time being. Andi wondered if she'd be able to coax that boy out again during this trip...and if she dared get close enough to try.

HEAVEN HELP HIM, Chance thought, if he allowed Andi to become a distraction. As he listened for an irregularity in the chug of the engines, he thought about the ease with which Andi clowned around with Nicole. Her sheer freedom of spirit mesmerized him. For that brief moment he'd forgotten everything but Andi, and it had been exhilarating. It had also been embarrassing to have Bowie catch him at it, yet again.

If Andi could capture his attention so completely when she wasn't even focusing on him, what would happen to his concentration if she turned that happy-go-lucky charm on him full force? He'd have to be damn careful this week.

Chance turned to Bowie. "You'd better go aft and tell me how I'm doing. When you give me the signal, I'll start backing."

Bowie paused. "Uh, Chance?"

"What?" Chance looked up impatiently.

"We're still tied to the dock."

Chance grimaced.

"I'll take care of it," Bowie said, heading toward the front deck.

Another lesson, Chance thought. He'd been so engrossed in thoughts of Andi he'd almost pulled half of the

Echo Bay dock out into the lake. God knows, the boat was big enough to do it.

"I think I'll go help him untie us," Andi said, following Bowie out onto the deck.

Chance watched her sashay through the door. The light played with her golden hair as she crouched to help Bowie with the thick ropes securing them to the dock. Just looking at her lifted his heart. And addled his brain.

"She's amazing," Nicole said, almost as if she could read the direction of his thoughts. "It's impossible to be depressed around her. She always searches out the fun side of life."

Chance looked over at Nicole. "I thought it was the younger one who was supposed to be wild and crazy."

Nicole laughed and waved a hand toward the front deck. "Tell that to her."

Chance looked outside again. Andi was swinging a rope like a lasso and threatening to hog-tie Bowie, who was pawing the ground and using his forefingers as horns.

"Don't underestimate her because she likes to kid around," Nicole said. "She'd go to the wall for the people she loves."

"Like Bowie."

"Yeah." Nicole smiled. "I recognized right away how alike they were. I'm sure that's what attracted me to him."

"I just wish he enjoyed his work at Jefferson more."

"Well, maybe if you could—" Nicole cut herself off as Andi and Bowie came back inside, flushed and laughing.

Chance felt an overwhelming urge to take Andi in his arms and kiss that laughing mouth. What a huge mistake that would be. "All set?" he asked.

Bowie snapped him a salute. "All secure and remarkably tight, Captain."

"Then get back there and protect my ass, Bowie."

"Aye, aye, Captain."

Nicole stood. "I'll go with you and help direct."

Bowie leered at her. "Trying to get me alone so you can have your way with me, aren't you?"

"Of course."

"Hot-diggity." Bowie guided Nicole down the passageway to the rear of the boat. "We'll be in the back making out, if you need us, Captain."

"Just don't embarrass the family," Chance called after them. He wished Andi had volunteered to go with Bowie instead of Nicole. That meant smart-mouthed Andi would be staying up front with him and be a witness to the disaster if he miscalculated and drove this barge into something. From the way she'd reacted to everything so far, he'd probably never live it down, either. He wiped his sweaty palms on his pants.

"Don't worry. You'll do fine," Andi said.

He glanced at her in surprise. Whatever he'd expected from her while he attempted this feat, it hadn't been moral support. "Thanks."

"I mean, what's the worst that could happen? You could wreck the boat, which is worth about a gabbillion dollars, by backing into someone else's boat, also worth about a gabbillion dollars, and both boats would sink in the middle of the harbor, making it impossible for anybody else to get in or out, and we'd all have to swim to the dock while crowds of people threw rotten food at us."

He chuckled. "Thanks for the encouraging words."

"Anytime." She smiled back.

He reached for his sunglasses and put them on, feeling

a little like Tom Cruise in *Top Gun*. He could by damn do this.

Bowie yelled the first command, and he put the boat in reverse. Funny thing, but his palms weren't sweating anymore.

SHE'D DONE IT, Andi thought as she sat on a bench seat where she could watch Chance at the wheel of the boat. She'd made him see the funny side of the situation and a little of the tension was gone from his jaw. And there were signs, small but significant, that he was loosening up. He hadn't acknowledged that Bowie had saved them from pulling off a section of the dock, though.

Slowly the boat slid out of the mooring slip, and when it had cleared, Chance muscled it around to the left with the help of instructions coming from Bowie in the back.

"You're clear. Punch it!" Bowie shouted.

The engines roared as Chance thrust the boat forward before it could drift toward the dock again. Bowie let out a rebel yell as the houseboat moved smoothly out of the marina.

"See?" Andi said. "Piece of cake."

He glanced at her. "Want to drive it?"

She was taken aback. "You mean that?"

"Sure, why not? Getting in and out of the marina has to be the worst of it. Just steer it along the shoreline. It's probably not much different than driving your van."

She stood and walked over to the captain's chair. As he began to explain the control panel to her, she caught another whiff of his cologne and her stomach did that funny little twisting trick again. *Face it, you're attracted to him.* She'd always been a sucker for a man with a nicely sculpted mouth and strong chin. That slight five-o'clock shadow she remembered from that first night in

Ginger's hallway was making its appearance again. Coupled with his flyboy sunglasses, it gave him a roguish air.

"Got it?"

She hadn't heard a word he'd been saying. "Got it."

"Then it's all yours," he said, sliding out of the chair and releasing the wheel.

She quickly took his place and put both hands on the wheel. The lake sparkled in front of her and the rocky coastline slipped by on her right. She adjusted to the motion of steering the boat. "Don't leave."

"I won't." He stood right behind her. "Ease over to the left. That outcropping looks like it extends into the water a ways. It sure helps that the water's so clear. You can see all the obstacles really easy."

"Too bad life isn't like that, huh?"

He sighed. "Yep."

That heartfelt sigh stirred her compassion. She was beginning to imagine what life might be like for the son of a dead business tycoon and a woman who sent a French teacher to instruct her unborn grandchild. Bowie had reacted by accepting the role of the reckless screwup, so nobody expected much of him, but Chance was just gritting it out, trying to carry the load for everyone.

Even through the engine noise she could pick out the sound of his breathing, and the steady rhythm gave her goose bumps. She fantasized what it would be like if they were on this boat by themselves, instead of sharing it with her sister and brother-in-law. She imagined Chance putting his arms around her and helping her steer as they navigated along the rocky shore. "How'm I doing?"

"Just fine." His voice sounded deeper than usual.

What a kick if he'd been having some of the same fantasies, she thought.

"Think you can handle it by yourself now?"

Her rosy fantasy collapsed. "I guess so. Got an important meeting to go to?"

"In a way. I want to change clothes, and I do have some calls to make while clients are still in their offices in New York. Plus, I want to see what the stock market did today."

"Couldn't you let it go for now? It's such a glorious afternoon."

"Can't."

"What's the worst that could happen? I'll bet the clients will still be around tomorrow, and if the stock market crashed, you might as well enjoy your evening, because you're in deep doo-doo, no matter what calls you make."

"First of all, the clients may not be around tomorrow. They might interpret my delay as lack of interest and do business with another company that's more enthusiastic. And the stock-market prices will affect what I say to my broker first thing in the morning, and I have tonight to consider my next move."

"It sounds exhausting. Don't you ever wish you could swim with the minnows for a change?"

"Did I hear somebody up here mention swimming?" Bowie said, coming into the living area. "Nicole's changing into her suit and mourning her lost figure, so I thought I'd—well, shiver me timbers, look who's driving the boat! Hey, Chance, want me to climb up to the roof and put out the distress flag to warn people out of our path?"

"She's doing fine," Chance said.

Andi warmed to the praise. "Watch your tongue, sailor," she said, "or the captain, who is yours truly at the moment, will order you flogged for insubordination."

"Cool. S and M," Bowie said.

Chance laughed.

"Hark!" Bowie said. "A strange sound fills the air.

Could it be? Is the Grand Pooh-Bah of Jefferson Sporting Goods—be still my heart—chortling?''

"I've never chortled in my life," Chance said, still laughing.

"Oh, yes. Chortling. In fact, there was the Great Chortle of 1975, when we snuck those turkeys into—"

"Nicole's out of the bathroom," Chance said, smoothly interrupting. "I'm changing clothes and making those calls."

"You just don't want Bowie to tell about the turkeys and spoil your image as a buttoned-down executive," Andi accused.

"That was a long time ago," he said. "You both will have to excuse me, but I have some work to do."

Andi waited until he left before she spoke. "He should have thanked you for remembering the ropes."

"What ropes? Oh, you mean untying us from the dock? That was no big deal."

"It would have been if you hadn't remembered."

"He probably didn't thank me because he's embarrassed that he forgot. He doesn't think he can afford a mistake, especially since Dad died. Once upon a time the guy knew how to have fun, but lately he's been nothing but old sobersides."

"Look, Bowie, I know you've engineered this trip partly to encourage him to relax, but he might not. Will you be okay with that?"

Bowie stared at the light dancing on the water. "I guess I won't have a choice," he said, his voice low. "But Andi, if he can't loosen up in a place like this, he's more of a mess than I thought."

"There's no such thing as an attractive maternity swimsuit," Nicole wailed as she came down the hallway and walked to the front of the boat so Andi could see her.

"Look at this, sis. I'm afraid if I go in the water somebody will try to harpoon me!"

Bowie rushed to her side and threw a protective arm in front of her. "I would *never* allow that, my love."

"Aw, Nic, you're very cute," Andi said. The loose-fitting white suit made Nicole look like an egg on stilts, but the effect was very endearing, especially when Andi considered that soon Nicole would have a baby girl for her troubles. Vanity didn't seem much of a price to pay for that. She wished their mother could have lived closer to take part in this pregnancy—she suspected Nicole missed that. "Motherhood looks good on you," she added, meaning every word.

"I absolutely agree," Bowie said gallantly, giving her a quick kiss.

"And it will all be worth it in two months," Andi said.

"You're right," Nicole said. "I haven't a complaint in the world, except that right now I would kill to get into that cool, clear water."

"Your wish is my command, love," Bowie said. He shaded his eyes and swept himself into a one-legged stance while he gazed off toward the continuous shoreline. "Land ho!"

"All ashore who's going ashore!" Andi decided it was time to take charge of the fun around here. "Sailor, go tell His Stuff-shirtedness that he's needed on the bridge. He can go commune with his laptop after we beach this sucker. It's time to party!"

4

TWO HOURS LATER, Andi, Bowie and Nicole sat on the rear deck in plastic deck chairs, their feet propped on the railing, and fishing poles dangling over the end of the boat. The prow was wedged firmly into the sand of a secluded little beach, and stout iron stakes held the mooring ropes for extra stability. Chance had taken the helm to run the boat aground and had helped Bowie drive the stakes into the sand and tie the mooring ropes. Soon afterward, he'd claimed he had reports to type and had disappeared inside the boat while the rest of them took a swim.

"We shoulda bought some live bait," Andi said, taking another sip of her beer. She and Bowie were indulging, while Nicole, the pregnant lady, had to settle for a soft drink.

"I agree," Nicole said. "These lures may be from Jefferson's finest stock, but the Lake Mead fish are not impressed."

"I want to try something," Bowie said, handing his fishing pole to Nicole. "Mind the line for me a little while. I'll be back."

"No problem. Nothing's biting anyway," Nicole said.

Andi was glad for the moment of privacy with her sister. She was determined to get Nicole's opinion about her latest career plan, but she didn't want Bowie or Chance, *especially* not Chance, throwing in their two cents worth.

"Listen, before he comes back, I want to talk about this idea I have."

"Please tell me this isn't about artificial insemination."

"What?"

"Don't do it, Andi. I've seen that longing look on your face, and that usually means you're about to try something crazy. I know this baby stuff looks like fun, but you don't have a steady income, and raising a kid alone would be hard enough if you had a lot of money, so—"

"Time out, Nic!" Andi braced her pole between her thighs and made a T with her hands. "The thought never crossed my mind."

"Never?"

"Well, okay, one time after we'd talked on the phone, and you were so excited about what color to paint the baby's room, and you'd just bought her first teddy bear, I *fleetingly* considered the possibility."

"Aha!"

"But I came to the same conclusions you just listed. I have to put my life together before I can think about bringing another life into the world. And I'd like to find a nice guy, too. Easier on me, easier on the kid." She smiled triumphantly at Nicole. "So there. Do I get points for that?"

Nicole wet her finger and drew three stripes on Andi's shoulder. "Well done, soldier."

"God, I remember how Dad used to do that. Remember when he started awarding us ranks?"

"Yeah, and you hated it because I usually outranked you."

"I think when he started assigning us ranks, I decided never to be that regimented. But...there comes a time... Don't laugh, but I'm thinking of expanding on yoga instruction and opening a school of my own, Nic."

"I'm not laughing. Would it take much capital?"

Andi gazed at her. "Spoken like the Nicole I know. Not *what a terrific idea,* but *would it take much capital?*"

"Isn't that why you're asking me, so I'll point out these things?"

Andi sighed. "I guess. And no, it wouldn't take much capital. I could build slowly, use creative ways to advertise. This is scary, but I'm actually thinking about a career, an honest-to-goodness vocation."

"My first reaction is that it sounds perfect for you. You're definitely the self-employment type."

"Thanks. I think so, too."

"And Mom will be *très* relieved to know you're not headed for the sperm bank."

"Mom thought I was about to get inseminated, too?"

Nicole adjusted her souvenir visor and looked at her. "She has some idea that you like to horn in on what I'm doing."

"I do not horn in."

"Remember the guppies?"

"The guppies weren't my fault!"

"Ha! Who dumped Jaws into the tank when I wasn't home? Maybe he was the hit man who wiped out Myrtle, Harry, Genevieve and Bernie, but you hired him."

"I thought an angel fish was a lot prettier than those dumb guppies. I just thought he'd show them up a little. I didn't know he'd eat them."

"Speaking of eating fish, I'm hoping to do that on this trip," Bowie said, plopping into the chair next to Nicole. "And I'm hoping we can catch something bigger than a guppy. So which one of you wants to help me try my new lure?" He held up two iridescent clusters of feathers and beads.

Nicole glanced at him. "Oh, Bowie, don't use those. I

promise to wear them really soon. They just take some getting used to.''

Andi gazed at the dazzle of colors. "Those are earrings? Fantastic!"

Bowie shrugged. "It was just an idea I had, so I made a pair for Nicole, but she really doesn't like them. She's more the pearl-and-diamond type."

"Not me," Andi said. "I think they're perfect, and you'll put them in the water over my dead body. Give them here."

Bowie handed them across Nicole with a smile of delight. "They're all yours."

Andi took out the red hoops in her ears and replaced them with the lure earrings. "What do you think?"

"They're you," Nicole said.

"Do you mean that in a good way or a bad way?"

"A good way." Nicole squeezed her knee. "After all, I trundled all the way out here just to get my Andi fix. The phone's okay, but I wanted a face-to-face."

"You miss not having Mom and Dad around, huh?"

Nicole nodded, and her eyes grew a little moist. "Damn, we're so spread out. I wish you two lived out here."

Bowie leaned back in his chair. "I could deal with living like this."

"I guess Chance can't," Andi said. "Is he still hunched over his laptop in there?"

"Sad but true," Bowie said.

Andi took another sip of her cold beer. "I can't imagine how he can stay inside, working on that stupid laptop when it's so gorgeous out here."

"To be honest, I didn't think he would, either. He used to love to fish," Bowie said. "It's almost as if he's deliberately avoiding being around us."

"That's weird."

"Yeah." Nicole gave Andi a speculative look. "Unless..."

"What? Why are you looking at me like that?"

"That red suit is dynamite on you."

"You're changing the subject."

"No, I'm not. You put that suit on while the guys were out staking the boat to the sand, remember?"

"Well, duh. It was the obvious chance to get naked without embarrassing anyone, so I grabbed it. We're not exactly loaded with privacy around here, in case you hadn't noticed. You'd think they'd put a few more doors on this thing."

"Yeah, I noticed. I also noticed Chance's reaction when you appeared in that swimsuit. The guy was salivating."

"He was?" Bowie said. "Hey, cool."

"I don't believe you," Andi said as a flush crept over her skin.

"Look at the facts," Nicole said. "It was right after you came out in the suit that he made some excuse about not feeling like a swim and went inside to work on those reports that suddenly became so important."

"They probably *were* really important, as far as he was concerned. The guy's driven," Andi said, but excitement stirred in her.

"I like the looks of this situation," Bowie said. "Day one, and we already have progress."

FEROCIOUS HUNGER PANGS and the aroma of grilling steak proved irresistible to Chance, and he stood and stretched, sniffing appreciatively. Switching off the laptop, he leaned down to peer outside. The sun glowed from behind a bank of clouds stretched across the horizon. A spectacular western sunset could be in the offing.

A sunset and a steak fry on the beach...with Andi. Now that he wasn't concentrating on his reports, he could hear laughter and a tape of some tropical-sounding music. He sighed. For the first time in years he had no idea what he was supposed to do. Oh, he knew very well what he wanted to do—become much better friends with the beauty in the red swimsuit. Yet despite his bachelor status, he didn't feel the least bit free. Jefferson Sporting Goods claimed his first loyalty, and the company was a jealous mistress.

Sometimes he could almost hear his father's voice. *The stockholders expect us to show a profit and still maintain stability, son. Take risks, but not foolish risks. Watch out for Bowie. He doesn't understand the difference.* There had been a heady joy in being the chosen one, the heir to the throne, but there was also a weight that seemed to get heavier every day. He'd never thought the day would come when he'd feel twinges of envy when he looked at Bowie's situation. He'd been wrong.

Watch out for Bowie. And although his father had never met Andi, no doubt he would have warned Chance to watch out for her, too. Still, he couldn't hold himself aloof for an entire week on this houseboat, just to avoid becoming involved with Andi. That would be boorish and rude. And he'd also starve to death.

He walked out the front sliding door and glanced at the beach. They'd taken four deck chairs down to the sand, and the empty fourth chair touched him. This afternoon they'd left him alone to do his work, but they obviously hoped he'd show up for dinner. He was so used to people wanting his company because of his position with Jefferson Sporting Goods that it was a revelation knowing someone wanted to spend time with him because they liked him.

They had the chairs arranged in a semicircle around a bed of embers where they were cooking the steaks. The chairs faced the sunset, which was just starting to pink up. They hadn't noticed him yet. Bowie still had on his trunks, but he'd added an unbuttoned shirt. Nicole got up to take a picture of him sitting in his chair, his beer can raised in a toast. Probably because she was self-conscious about her protruding belly, she'd put a filmy cover-up over her bathing suit. Bowie and Nicole looked relaxed and happy, and his heart swelled with love for them.

A more potent emotion hit him as he studied Andi in her red suit and sarong-type skirt. She crossed her legs and the flowered skirt fell away, revealing her smooth thighs. Chance swallowed. Well, it wasn't going to get any easier, so he might as well go down. He took off his deck shoes, opened the metal gate at the prow of the boat and leaped the short distance to the sand.

"Ahoy and avast, matey!" Bowie called, raising his can of beer again. "The grog isn't half-bad in these climes."

"The company's not so bad, either," Nicole said.

"The fishing sucks," Andi said, "but the grog and the company make up for it."

"I figured the fishing wasn't working out when I smelled steak," Chance said, walking through the sand to the available chair, which was right next to Andi's.

Bowie pulled a beer out of a cooler and tossed it to him. "Andi picked out the brewskies, and let me tell you, the woman knows her beer."

"A highly sought-after talent," Andi said.

Chance popped the top and took a drink. "Good stuff." He glanced at Andi, then looked closer. She'd swept her hair up on top of her head, and dangling from both ears were what looked like fishing lures. "Are those hooks in your ears on purpose, or are you the victim of Bowie's lousy casting skills?"

"Hey," Bowie said. "Just because I happened to hook a woman's cheek once, which really wasn't—"

"Ew, Bowie!" Nicole made a face. "How awful! You could have blinded her!"

"It wasn't her face," Chance said. "And she was wearing a string bikini at the time."

"Oh," Nicole said. "Still, that makes me wince, Bowie. I hope now you're more careful when you cast."

"That's just it. I wasn't casting. We were out on a charter fishing boat, and everybody else was in shorts and shirts except this Bo Derek clone. I think she was after bigger fish than the ones in the water, if you get my drift. I was bringing in my line, and here she comes, wiggling along listening to *Bolero* on her headset, I suppose. I got a little discombobulated, and next thing I know, my hook's in her butt."

"Oh." Nicole glanced at him. "That does sound kind of stupid on her part. Who was this bimbo?"

"Chance's date."

"Ooo-wee!" Andi threw back her head and laughed. "He got you back, Chance." Then she flashed him a look that heated his blood. "Better not mess with the Bowie-man."

"Good advice." Chance took a long swallow of his beer, which quenched at least one thirst he was feeling. He remembered that woman he'd asked out on the fishing trip. He hadn't known her very well. Matter of fact, that was the problem with most of the women he'd dated recently. To get to know someone, you needed to spend time with them, and he hadn't had that kind of time.

"To answer your question about the decorations in my earlobes, they're earrings Bowie made. Take a look." She leaned toward him, bringing her coconut-oil scent close enough to make him dizzy.

He wanted to nibble on her ear instead of examining her earring. "That's not an actual lure, is it?" Even as he said it, he realized it was a lure of a different kind, dancing feathers and beads capable of hooking him, but good.

"Nah, it's not the real thing," Bowie said. "I just put together stuff I thought looked pretty. Nicole wasn't wild about them. But Andi loves 'em, so I gave them to her."

"I do love them." Andi settled back in her chair and raised her beer can to her full lips. "Hey, everybody, sunset alert. The sky's on fire."

"Wow," Nicole said. "I'd forgotten how spectacular the sunsets are around here."

Chance sipped his beer and listened to the sound of steel drums coming from the tape deck. Red and gold unfurled in the sky, spilling over the mountains and into the water.

"It's like looking through rose-colored glasses, isn't it?" Andi said in a voice so soft only he would have been able to hear.

He glanced over at Bowie and Nicole. They were holding hands and leaning close, caught up in their own private love fest. "It's also like watching a giant fingerpainting being made," he said.

"I like that," Andi said, giving him a smile. "I used to love fingerpaints."

"Me, too."

She was silent for a while as the colors slowly faded to brick and a few stars winked on. "When was the last time you fingerpainted?" she asked finally.

"Thirty years ago." Funny how he could still remember the claylike scent of the paint and the cool squish of the colors beneath his hands. He'd used his palms, his knuckles, even his wrists to make designs.

"I wish I'd bought some to bring on this trip."

"I think our niece is still a little young, don't you?" He'd meant it as a joke, but the minute he said the *our niece* part he got a tingle of awareness. Uncle Chance. Aunt Andi. They'd be linked together even more closely once this child was born. He felt himself sinking deeper into inevitability.

"I meant fingerpaints for us," Andi said. "It would've been a fun thing to do this week."

"Yeah, I can picture you and Bowie getting into that."

"I wasn't picturing Bowie. I was picturing you."

He grew uneasy. "Oh, yeah, right," he said sarcastically.

"Why not?"

"Because it's too childish for me now." He winced at how crude his response had sounded. "Sorry. That didn't come out right. I meant that—"

"You meant exactly what you said. But the thing is, I'm not insulted at all. As a matter of fact, I feel sorry for you."

That brought him out of his chair. "*Sorry* for me?" He faced her. "What in hell do you mean by that crack?"

"Chance, watch out," she said.

"Ah, the peaceful tranquillity of twilight," Bowie said. "The call of a nightbird. The indignant shout of my brother."

"She feels sorry for me because I don't want to fingerpaint!" Chance said, backing up.

Andi started to get out of her chair. "Chance, don't—" Her skirt caught on the arm of her chair, pulling the chair over and knocking her off balance, toward him.

As he stumbled backward in the process of trying to catch her and stay upright at the same time, he tripped over some rocks and figured they'd both land on the ground. Miracle of miracles, he staggered but stayed vertical, and so did she. Maybe his luck was changing. He released her with a sigh of relief at another disaster averted. "She feels sorry for me," he said to Bowie and Nicole. "Can you beat that?"

"Sure," Bowie said, standing. "I feel sorry for all of us. You just backed into the grill. Our steaks are in the coals."

"Oh, hell." Chance turned to the fire. Instinctively he reached to grab a sizzling piece of meat and singed his fingers. "Dammit!" He stuck his fingers in his mouth. So much for changed luck.

"Here's a barbecue fork," Andi said, waving the pronged instrument dangerously close to him.

"Keep your distance, woman!" Chance held up both hands. "Next thing I know, I'll be impaled on that thing."

"I was trying to warn you about the fire! Do you need first aid?"

"Mustard's the best thing to put on it," Nicole said, getting out of her chair with a small groan. "I'll—"

"No, I'll get it," Bowie said. "After two beers I'd need a crane to help me hoist you back on the barge, sweetheart."

"Bowie Jefferson, you take that back!"

"Yeah, Bowie," Andi said. "You try smuggling a watermelon and see how spry you are."

"My apologies, ladies." Bowie swept them a bow and went over to kiss his wife on the cheek. She glared at him. "Chance, buddy, I think we might want to retreat to the boat, get your fingers taken care of, and return with more libations and the salad while these gorgeous, *petite,* talented women pull our steaks from the fire. Maybe if we're lucky, they'll find it in their hearts to let us eat dinner by the time we get back.''

''Don't count on it,'' Nicole called after them as they trudged through the sand.

Chance followed Bowie toward the boat. ''Hey, I'm sorry I knocked the steaks into—'' Sharp pain interrupted his apology as his toe collided with a piece of driftwood. ''Dammit!''

''What?''

''Stubbed my toe.''

''I guess it's been a long time since you've walked barefoot on the beach, huh, buddy? You gotta watch where you're going.''

''Bowie, right now I feel as if I'm standing in the middle of a damn minefield.''

''Just relax, buddy. You're among friends.''

''And some are more dangerous than others,'' Chance muttered.

5

ANDI WAS SO HUNGRY that she didn't even care that the steak tasted like charcoal on the outside. Everyone balanced their plates on their lap. After attempts to cut the steak with a knife and fork nearly tipped her plate upside down in the sand, Andi picked up the piece of meat in her fingers. "If it was good enough for my ancestors, it's good enough for me," she said, biting into the steak.

"Fine for those of you who have working fingers," Chance said. Bowie had wrapped three of his with gauze.

"I happen to know you can drive with one hand," Bowie said. "I'll bet you can eat one-handed, too."

"Ah, yes," Nicole said. "The old one-handed driving technique. The left hand for the steering wheel, the right hand for taking liberties with us, your dates. I remember it well."

"And they always thought they were being so subtle," Andi said. "They'd be staring straight ahead, like they didn't even know you were there in the car. But the hand would come creeping over like Thing in 'The Addams Family.'"

"You wanted us to *look* at you?" Chance said. "We're not about to take our eyes off the road and risk wrapping our pride and joy around a telephone pole."

"Yeah," Andi said, laughing, "and you might wreck the car, too." She noticed that Chance was on his second beer, and it was having a good effect. He was definitely loosening up. If she could just avoid another mishap, she could build on that. "I'm going down to the lake to wash my hands. Anybody else need to do that?"

"I'll just lick my fingers," Chance said.

"If I play my cards right, I can get Nicole to lick my fingers," Bowie said.

"In your dreams, Romeo," Nicole said. "Andi, would you bring me back a wet napkin? I don't think I can move from this spot."

"Anything for you, toots." Andi grabbed a couple of napkins and stood.

"You're tired, my little cabbage?" Bowie asked Nicole.

"Exhausted. Don't forget, it's two hours later, Chicago time. It's been a long day for a pregnant lady."

"Then I guess dancing wild and barefoot on the sand is out," Bowie said.

"Get Andi to dance with you," Nicole said as Andi started down toward the lake.

"What about Chance?" Bowie asked.

"Get him to dance with you, too. Just let me sit and digest that charred steak in peace."

Andi hadn't considered the prospect of dancing on the beach. Would Chance finally abandon his sedate corporate image, or would he let Bowie be the life of the party, as usual? This night could get very interesting indeed.

She walked to the edge of the lake, the sand cool under her feet near the waterline, and discovered that the lake was filled with stars.

Fascinated, she rippled the water with her fingers and watched the stars become streaks of light, like a thousand comets dashing across the liquid surface. Then she looked up and found that she was standing under a bowl of stars reaching all the way to the horizon. Overcome with the beauty of it, she reached her arms up to the sky. "Hallelujah!"

"Amen, sister!" Bowie called back.

"Have you chowhounds looked up from your plates long enough to notice all these stars?" Andi asked.

"They're gorgeous, Andi," Nicole said.

"But nothing compared to you, my sweet Nicole," Bowie said.

"Cool it, Bowie. I'm not dancing with you, and that's that."

"It's as if Liberace swirled his cape over the sky," Andi said, staring upward until her neck hurt.

"Let me know if you see Elvis walking across the lake," Bowie said. "In the meantime, I'm putting on a dance tape. Despite my heavy-lidded wifelet, the Lake Mead Jefferson Houseboat Party is just getting started."

As Andi dipped napkins in the lake, the sound of marimbas and guitars filled the air. She smiled as she listened to Bowie trying to get Nicole to dance with him.

"Aw, come on, Nic. One little turn around the sand," Bowie coaxed.

"Forget it, Fred Astaire. Head on down the line."

Andi turned just as Bowie gyrated rhythmically over to where Chance sat.

"May I have this dance?" he asked, still holding his beer in one hand.

To Andi's amazement, Chance got to his feet. Taking occasional swigs of his beer, he started executing a credible cha-cha with his brother.

"Ooh, have we got style!" Bowie cried. "Have we got rhythm!"

"Have you drunk way too much beer!" Nicole said, laughing.

Andi stood, the wet napkins dripping on her bare feet,

almost afraid to move for fear the spell Chance was under would break and he'd make some excuse to go type reports again.

"Come on, Andi!" Bowie called, whirling in her direction and snatching the wet napkins. "Cut in."

Breathless and smiling, she entered the dance in Bowie's place. All she could see of Chance's face in the dim light was the white flash of his grin as he matched his steps to hers. They didn't touch, yet they seemed to know when to pivot, when to turn in time with each other, as if they'd been dancing this way for years.

The small space between their bodies crackled and snapped in time to the rhythm. Andi forgot everything but the music and the sensuous movements of the man across from her. His transformation, no matter how temporary, had completely captured her imagination.

Then the music changed to something slower and more languorous.

Vaguely she heard Bowie's plea and Nicole's weary agreement to dance the slow number with him. One dance.

For a heart-stopping moment, neither Chance nor Andi moved. Then he stepped forward and drew her slowly into his arms, the empty beer can cradled against the small of her back as he wrapped both arms around her in the casual dance position of lovers. She wound her arms around his neck and breathed in the tangy scent of beer mixed with his sexy aftershave.

Their bodies moved with the lazy rhythm of the music, but she could feel the rapid tattoo of his heart against her breast, and her own heart was racing out of control. Of course, they'd just been doing a very athletic cha-cha. Of course, that was the reason. Not.

She lifted her head to look up at him. He gazed down

at her. She could barely see his shadowed eyes, yet she knew he was looking intently into her face. All that intensity he'd focused on his business was now trained on her like a laser, and she had trouble breathing. The twist of desire in her stomach grew stronger with each moment she spent swaying in his arms.

His head dipped lower. Her lips parted in anticipation. She closed her eyes.

Then another set of arms enfolded both of them. "Just carry on," Bowie said, one arm around each of them as he swayed with the dance rhythm. "Nicole's really dead on her feet. We're turning in."

The magic between Chance and Andi shattered like starlight on the lake when a pebble was tossed in.

"Good idea," Chance said, backing away from Andi as Bowie and Nicole headed for the boat.

"Yeah, we've all had a big day," Andi said. She could have cheerfully killed Bowie with her bare hands. "You guys all go ahead. We have to take turns in the bathroom, anyway. I'll stay out here and do a few yoga routines. Can't abandon my practice, you know."

Chance paused. "Is that right?"

"Well, sure. You have to stay toned, stay flexible, especially if you're a role model for other people."

He gazed at her as if the concept hadn't occurred to him.

She felt slightly insulted. "You're not the only one who has to think about work sometimes."

"I guess not. Well, good night." He turned and headed for the boat where Nicole was trying to hoist herself up to the deck with Bowie's help. "Hey, newlyweds. Let Uncle Chance help." He leaped to the deck in one smooth motion and lifted Nicole from above while Bowie steadied her from below.

"I *hate* being so awkward," Nicole complained.

"Bowie and I consider it a privilege to help you," Chance said as he drew her up beside him.

"You're sweet." She patted his cheek. "Why don't you go back and dance with Andi some more? I didn't mean to break up the party."

Andi held her breath. The music still played on the tape deck.

"I think it's time we all turned in," Chance said.

Andi walked over and shut off the music.

CLOSE CALL, Chance thought as he switched on his laptop and tried to concentrate on some spreadsheets while Bowie and Nicole got ready for bed. If Bowie hadn't interrupted him, he'd have kissed Andi. It would have been so easy. Bowie would have been thrilled with that, doggone his matchmaking hide.

Watch out for Bowie. No kidding, Chance thought. Here he was doing his damnedest to keep a level head, and Bowie springs Andi on him. Just thinking about the warmth and softness of her body moving rhythmically against his made him ache. He wouldn't think about it, or he was liable to go back out there.

The beer had probably lowered his resistance. He'd give it up for this week. He'd totally underestimated the power of her attraction, and the unconscious—or maybe conscious—provocation of her movements. When she'd stood down by the lake, her womanly figure silhouetted by stars, he'd begun to want her with a fierceness that swept aside all reservation.

And when she'd come willingly into his arms for a slow dance...when she'd lifted her mouth so invitingly...

The laptop beeped and the spreadsheet disappeared from the screen. Chance straightened on the bench seat and pressed a few buttons, but the spreadsheet was no longer on the menu. In his clumsiness with the gauze bandages and his preoccupation with Andi, he'd deleted it.

"Dammit!" He exited the program before he could do any more damage.

"What's wrong?" Bowie said, coming out of the bathroom with a toothbrush in one hand.

Chance grimaced. "Nothing a brain transplant wouldn't solve."

"Is it a problem with Jefferson?"

"Yeah. Chauncey M. Jefferson the Fourth, to be specific."

Bowie came over and sat opposite him. "I screwed up big-time by interrupting your dance with Andi."

"Even matchmakers miscalculate, thank God."

"Damn. We should have just quietly slipped away."

"Oh, right. You should have silently hoisted Nicole four feet off the ground and heaved her onto the boat without either of you making a peep."

"She is getting to be a load, isn't she? And still two months to go. It's going to be a giant kid."

"We should always use two of us to get her in and out of the boat, so nobody gets hurt."

"Keep your voice down. She still hasn't forgiven me for saying essentially the same thing."

"Not quite. You mentioned the need for a crane. Women get touchy at a time like this."

"So speaketh the expert on pregnant ladies. Is there anything you're not an expert on?"

"A few things." Chance glanced out into the night, where Andi still presented a huge temptation.

"Go back out there. Turn on the music. Andi's a great gal, and I think it would do you a world of good to spend some time alone with her."

Chance eyed his brother. "Forget it. I had a momentary lapse. It won't happen again."

"I know I'm not imagining things. You're attracted to her. Go with it."

"Doesn't matter. If you took the time to think it through, you'd see what a mistake it would be for all of us if I get involved with her. She belongs out here, in the wild and woolly west. I'm tied to Chicago, so the relationship couldn't go anywhere. The most likely scenario is that we'd have a fling and split, which would make the family dynamics even worse than before."

"I don't know. Andi might relocate to Chicago. She misses Nicole a lot, and with their parents always on the move, the two of them really depend on each other."

Chance refused to allow himself a smidgen of hope. "If Andi wanted to be closer to Nicole, she would have moved by now. It's not as if she has a skyrocketing career going here in Nevada. My guess is she likes the weather and the lifestyle."

"Dammit, Chance, this seems like a good shot at having a relationship. Dad wouldn't have expected you to become a monk."

"No, but he sure as hell would expect me to find somebody who'd genuinely want to be a corporate wife. That's not Andi."

Bowie frowned. "Unfortunately, you might have a point there."

"And that's why I'm not going back down to the beach. Not tonight or any night this week."

"I still think you're making assumptions that might not be true." Bowie stood to leave. "Sleep tight, buddy." He started to walk away and turned back. "Like I have to remind you." He went into the bathroom and closed the door.

Chance sighed. Bowie was still Bowie, spouting his favorite philosophy—live for the moment and never face the facts. He walked over to the seat where Bowie had been sitting and unfolded it. For the first time he noticed how quiet the night was without traffic noise and the scream of sirens. Somewhere in the bushes at the edge of the beach a cricket chirped, but that was the extent of the excitement. He hoped to God he'd be able to sleep.

A half hour later he lay in the dark, listening to the same damn cricket. A musician it wasn't. Same monotonous tune over and over.

He couldn't blame the cricket for his insomnia, though. He'd realized after turning out the light that Andi would have to walk right past him when she came in. He needed to remind her to lock the door after her. Yeah, that was why he was still awake. She might forget.

No, that wasn't it. He might as well admit that he worried about the door lock because it was a safe topic. Worrying about whether he'd speak to her, whether he'd reach for her, whether he'd pull her down to this bed and kiss those full lips—that wasn't safe. He got up and put his shorts back on, as if they'd act as some sort of chastity belt.

Then he heard an unfamiliar noise. He sat up. There it was again, and it was no cricket. He knew that yoga involved chanting, but this was no chant, either. More like an obnoxious drunk braying at the moon. Andi was out there, vulnerable to whatever lunatic might be prowling the beach.

His feet hit the floor and he barked his shin on the edge of the bed. Swearing under his breath, he grabbed the barbecue fork from the table and barreled out the front door onto the deck. "Andi?"

She was sitting cross-legged in the sand, facing the bushes. She turned and glanced up at him. "Shh."

For one wild moment he wondered if she'd made the noise herself, as part of some mystic pagan ritual, but then it came again, from the direction of the bushes.

Andi might think safety lay in silence, but hiding from danger wasn't Chance's style. Wielding the fork, he leaped to the sand. "Who's out there?" he shouted. "Show yourselves or get the hell out of here!"

There was a snort and the clatter of hooves. *Hooves?* Damn drunks must have been riding horses.

"Hey!" Andi protested, getting to her feet. "You scared them."

"That was the idea." He was breathing hard and his heart pounded from the adrenaline rush. "You'd better come over here, closer to me, in case they circle around and come back."

"They wouldn't hurt us."

He stared at her. "What's that, some New Age trust in your fellow humans? Some drunken bastards riding around the lake on horses don't sound like the kind of company we want around here. This isn't the Old West, y'know, where you invite any passing saddle tramp to share your campfire."

She began to smile. "They were burros."

"Okay, drunks riding burros. That doesn't make them any less suspicious, in my opinion. You saw how they took off, acting guilty as hell. They were up to something."

"Nobody was riding the burros," she said, her smile widening. "They're wild. The sound you heard was them braying."

He mentally replayed the noise he'd heard. "I thought donkeys went hee-haw."

Her shoulders shook and she covered her mouth with one hand. "It's not quite that neat a sound." She cleared her throat. "It's more like *eeagh-haugh!*"

"You do that very well."

"Thank you." She continued to grin at him. "I guess you've never heard a real one."

"No." He glanced down at the fork he still clutched in his hand. It was tough to imagine how he could have made a bigger fool of himself than by charging out of the house-boat ready to battle wild burros with a barbecue fork.

"It was really sweet of you to be so ready to defend me, though."

He grimaced and walked over to toss the fork back up on the deck. "From fuzzy little burros."

"You thought it was a band of drunken desperadoes, and you were ready to take them on with a barbecue fork. That's pretty gallant."

He turned back to her. "Oh, I'm a regular Lone Ranger."

She walked up to him. "I think you are, at that. All the cares of the world rest on those Armani-covered shoulders, don't they, Chance?"

He shrugged, trying to remain calm. She was danger-ously close, and the adrenaline rush seemed to be meshing with a different kind of jolt to his system. He'd be wise to end this little conversation before things got out of hand. "Somebody has to be the grown-up."

"Twenty-four hours a day?" Her bathing-suit-covered breasts lightly nudged his bare chest as she moved closer still.

"You can't just turn it on and off."

She slid a cool hand behind his neck. "Isn't there an override switch somewhere?"

He closed his eyes. Her touch was like velvet against

his suddenly hot skin. She spread her fingers and ran them lightly up through his hair. He drew in a breath.

Then she applied subtle pressure to the back of his head, urging him down. "Kiss me, Chance. Trip that override switch."

6

ANDI HAD ALREADY hot-wired his override switch, Chance thought, winding his arms around her and opening his eyes long enough to make sure his mouth would connect solidly with hers. He felt her lips part beneath his hungry assault, and the muffled groan that filled his throat sounded the death knell of his restraint.

She took the first thrust of his tongue with an urgency that sent the blood pounding straight to his groin. He pulled her closer, wanting her to feel the pressure of his erection. The coconut scent of her suntan oil mingled with the scent of arousal, his and hers. Finally he accepted the truth—he'd wanted this from the first moment he saw her seven months ago. Maybe she'd wanted the same thing.

She tasted forbidden and lush. The sensual movement of her hips told him she was ready for anything he had in mind, and his mind raced with images of hands stroking, mouths exploring, bodies joining in pulsing completion.

His lips sought the honey from her warm mouth as he wedged his pelvis firmly between her thighs. She moaned and pushed against him, blotting out all reason.

He reached for the shoulder strap of the red suit that had tantalized him for hours. The strap offered no obstacle as it slipped down her smooth shoulder. Pushing his throbbing erection against the cradle of her thighs, he abandoned her lips to seek the pulse at her throat. His heart hammered as he worked the bathing suit down and finally cupped her breast in his hand.

She arched her back, pushing up against his palm. She was matching him desire for desire, and he'd never felt so excited by a woman in his life. She moaned as he leaned down and took her nipple into his mouth. He rolled the sensitive tip against his tongue and felt her shudder. Ah, this was going to be good. Very, very good.

He pulled the other strap down so he had access to both breasts as she writhed and whimpered against him. He felt her warm breath on the back of his leg. Dimly he realized that would be difficult, given their upright position. He paused.

Someone, or some*thing*, was breathing on him. He lifted his mouth from her breast.

Andi grew still in his arms. "Chance." Her voice held a warning.

The warm air traveled up the back of his legs. Every hair on his body stood erect. "What's breathing on me?" he whispered.

"A burro."

"*Shi—*"

She clamped her arms tight around his shoulders. "Don't make any sudden moves."

He leaned his forehead against hers and tried to stay calm. At least he wasn't naked. "Do they bite?"

"I don't know."

"That's not the right answer."

"Just stand still."

"Easy for you to say," he muttered. "It's not licking your leg."

"Licking?"

"Yeah. Probably for the salt, but God, it tickles."

"I'm going to try something. Stay still." She leaned around him. "Shoo!"

He stared down at her. "Shoo?"

"You got anything better?"

"Yeah. I'm going to turn around really fast and yell at him. Stay behind me."

"I don't know if that's a good idea."

"I do. He's started nibbling on my shorts."

"Then it must be a female."

"Ha, ha. Okay, on three. One, two, three, *now!*" He whirled and shoved her behind him. His eyes widened as he gazed at not one, but *four* burros. "Go home!" he yelled, waving one arm as he kept the other behind him, protecting Andi.

The burros trotted away a couple of yards and stood looking at him.

Andi started to laugh.

"What's so funny?"

"They *are* home. We're the trespassers."

"Oh. Okay, then go...somewhere else!" he yelled again, waving his arm some more.

Andi whipped off her sarong and stepped out from behind him. "Shoo!" she said, waving the skirt at them.

The flapping cloth seemed to do the trick. They spooked and took off into the bushes.

Chance stared after them, shaking his head. "Burros."

"Now that they know interesting stuff is here, they might come back."

He glanced at her. She was sliding her arms into the straps of her swimsuit.

The burros had broken the spell that had caused him to forget everything except the need to make love to her, but sanity had returned, and he was flabbergasted at his behavior. What had he been thinking? "Do you realize what almost happened?"

She smiled at him. "I think so. I watched all the films in junior-high health class."

"Exactly. And in those films, do you remember that little matter of taking precautions?"

She paused and gave him a long look. "You don't have anything with you?"

"No. Why would I have anything? This was supposed to be a family vacation. I didn't even know you were coming along, and I wouldn't have brought birth control even if I had known. Our last meeting wasn't exactly romantic."

"But I thought guys always carried something."

"Well, they don't. And even if I had something, what kind of guy would have grabbed a condom on his way out to save you?"

"One who expected me to be very grateful?"

He laughed in spite of himself and shook his head. "Oh, boy."

"So you would have made love to me without using anything?"

"Looks like it, doesn't it?"

"Hmm." She gave him a slow smile.

"What's that supposed to mean?"

"It's nice to know Chance Jefferson isn't quite as buttoned-down as he pretends."

He rubbed the back of his neck. He didn't like being at a disadvantage, and he always seemed to get in that position with Andi. "I'd appreciate it if you'd keep this little incident just between us."

"Of course."

"Thanks."

"What shall we do now?" she asked.

"Go to bed—separately."

"Well, that's pretty obvious, but what about the rest of the week?"

"Andi, we're on a houseboat with two other people. I went crazy enough to want to make love out here on the sand, but obviously that has certain…hazards. And I don't know about you, but even if we had birth control, I wouldn't feel very comfortable getting wild and crazy inside the houseboat, with Nicole and Bowie just down the hall. The only doors on this barge are for closets and the bathroom. Neither place seems appropriate, so I think it's a moot point."

"That stinks."

"To be honest, it probably saves us from making a terrible mistake."

"It didn't feel like a terrible mistake a little while ago. If you're so intent on being honest, why don't you admit it felt damn good, Chance?"

And it still would, he thought, watching her standing there, her breasts thrust forward in defiance. He remembered how the blood had raced in his veins when she'd arched into his caress. "I want you, Andi," he said quietly. "After this, I can't very well pretend not to. But our lives don't fit together, and all we can do is hurt each other. That's not going to promote family harmony, and I don't think either of us wants to make difficulties for Bowie and Nicole."

"Ah, I see, the reasonable, responsible Chance is back in control."

"Barely."

"Well, that's something." She turned and hoisted herself up on deck. "Good night, Chance."

He watched her go, and then he swore under his breath. For the first time in his life, he truly resented the wealth and position life had settled on him. Had he been the only one to consider, he would have figured a way around all the obstacles. He would have made love to Andi Lombard.

"HEY, the stock market rebounded last night!"

Chance's enthusiastic announcement from somewhere in the front of the boat woke Andi up.

"Bully," she muttered. "Better than an orgasm anytime, right, Chance, old boy?" She'd gone to sleep frustrated and had awakened in the same condition, although the smell of bacon and coffee coming from the kitchen helped mollify her. From the sound of things, everybody was up except her. Waves slapped the side of the boat and a breeze blew through the tiny window over her bunk. She peered out at a cloudy day and choppy gray water.

Hopping down from the top bunk, she located her duffel bag in the stash of supplies on the bottom bunk and went into the bathroom to change into her spare bathing suit. Acting so impulsively with Chance had been a stupid move, she thought as she took off her nightie and put on the suit. Recently, she'd vowed to start looking before she leaped into romantic encounters. Maybe then she'd find herself kissing Mr. Right instead of the usual Mr. Wrong.

The black tank-style suit might be a tad provocative, she thought as she glanced in the bathroom mirror. A lace insert down the front and each side didn't leave much to the imagination. But what woman deliberately bought a suit that made her look sexless? Mother Teresa, maybe. Not Andi Lombard. Chance would just have to deal with his hormones, she decided, walking out into the kitchen.

Bowie looked up from the bacon he was turning with a familiar-looking barbecue fork. "He-ere's Andi!"

"Morning. Did every—"

"Oh, God!" Chance wailed from the table which had become his temporary office. "Quick, throw me a towel, somebody."

Andi grabbed a towel from the kitchen counter and threw it at his head with a certain amount of relish. He caught it and started mopping his keyboard.

Nicole slid down from her perch on the captain's chair and went over to watch. "What happened, Chance?"

"Spilled my coffee."

Bowie paused with the fork in midair. Then he turned to give Andi the once-over. "Uh-huh. Wonder what came over him? Any ideas, Andi, sweetheart?" He winked at her. "Nice suit, by the way."

Nicole looked over at Andi and back at Chance. She grinned. "It is a nice suit, don't you think, Chance?"

"Didn't notice," he mumbled.

Bowie leaned closer to Andi. "He didn't notice," he said in a stage whisper. "It was pure coincidence that the minute you came into the room, he started pouring his coffee into his computer."

"I guess I'll just have to let it dry out and hope it still works." Chance picked up the open laptop as if it were an injured animal and carried it out to the front deck.

Nicole clapped her hands together. "I *love* it. I haven't seen him this rattled since he got showered with champagne at our reception. I wish I'd seen his face when you first walked in just now. I'll bet his jaw was on the floor."

Andi looked down at the black suit. "Is it too much? I'm beginning to get a complex. Every time I'm around, something crazy happens to Chance."

"It's time a few crazy things happened to Chance," Bowie said. "The guy needs to have his chain rattled. Now, if anyone cares to scramble up a few eggs, the bacon's about ready."

"I'll do it," Nicole said.

"Nope. I will. You relax." Andi opened the refrigerator and took out a carton of eggs. "How did you sleep last night?"

"Unfortunately, your niece kicked most of the night, so I didn't sleep a lot."

Andi paused in the midst of closing the refrigerator door. "That's too bad." She wondered if Nicole had heard what had gone on in the sand outside the boat the night before.

Chance came back in. "I put the laptop on a deck chair outside, but turned it away from the sun. I think it'll dry quicker that way than leaving it in here."

"I wouldn't know," Nicole said, "but it sounds logical. I'd offer you a hair dryer, but I didn't bring one. Did you, Andi?"

"Nope." She stood next to Bowie and cracked eggs into a bowl while butter melted in a frying pan "I figured I wasn't on this trip to be gorgeous."

Bowie lowered his voice. "Just sexy as hell."

She answered out of the corner of her mouth as she whipped the eggs. "These are the suits I happen to have, okay?" She poured the eggs into the frying pan.

"Very okay. He's a basket case."

"By the way, I heard those crazy wild burros braying last night," Nicole said. "And you tearing out to save Andi, Chance."

Andi froze. Sound tended to carry in such an open area. How much else had Nicole heard? Not that there had been much talking. Moaning and gasping, but not much conversation.

She turned, a spatula in her hand. "Yeah, it was very sweet, Nic. He'd never heard what real burros sound like, and he thought some drunks were out there having a party.

I explained it, and that was that. It's nice to know chivalry isn't dead.'' She didn't look at Chance.

"It's nice to know my brother isn't, either," Bowie said.

Andi kicked him. "Eggs are ready."

During breakfast they plotted the cruising for the day. Andi sat across from Chance. She couldn't help noticing that he seemed intent on keeping his gaze on her face whenever he looked in her direction. Even then, there was a banked heat in his blue eyes that made her stomach flutter every time she saw it. His hormones were definitely giving him problems. But then, so were hers.

"I hope the weather doesn't deteriorate," Nicole said, glancing at the cloudy sky outside the windows as they cleared away the dishes.

"It's not supposed to rain this week," Andi said. "But we might have wind."

"Then we'll just find a sheltered little cove and wait it out," Bowie said. "Before we break up camp, though, I want Andi to teach me a couple of yoga moves."

"Seriously?"

"I'm a man of many facets," Bowie said. "And yoga's always intrigued me. Maybe after we finish the dishes, we can—"

"I'll do the dishes," Chance said. "You two go ahead."

"And what am I supposed to do?" Nicole asked.

"Be pregnant," Andi said, giving her a hug. "Go lie down in the back for a little while. If you didn't sleep much last night, you probably could use some more rest."

Nicole looked relieved. "Thanks. Maybe I will, at that."

After she left, Chance turned to Bowie. "Is she okay?"

"She says she's fine. The baby's just being especially

active, that's all. I told her we'd cut the trip short anytime she wanted to, but she wouldn't hear of it."

"She's really looked forward to this week," Andi said. "It would be a huge disappointment if we had to go home early, but we have to think about her health, too."

"We won't go far from the marina today, just in case," Chance said. "And don't forget, I have the cell phone if we have an emergency."

"Let's hope the stock market isn't closing when we need to use it," Bowie said.

Chance gave him a lazy smile in response. "Have I increased your personal investments in the last six months or haven't I?"

"Yeah, but I'm a little worried about that ticker tape that's started coming out of your ear every morning." Bowie's smile was just as lazy, but there was an edge to it.

"I'm surprised you noticed. The laugh track that runs constantly in your brain must drown out everything else."

"Boys, boys." Feeling like a dorm mother, Andi stepped between them. Her father would have suggested these two put on the gloves and go a few rounds to work out their frustrations with each other. He'd even tried that technique a couple of times when she and Nicole had been bickering, until their mother had protested that he was raising a couple of brawlers. "Come on, Bowie. I'll teach you the salute to the sun."

"What sun? It's cloudy."

"So maybe we'll coax it out." She gave him a steely stare. "And do not *ever* question the master, grasshopper. Always remember, you are but a speck of bug dung on the windshield of humanity."

"You're not the first person to offer that opinion."

Andi had been kidding, but she wished she could pull

the joke back. No doubt when his father had told him something similar, he'd been deadly serious. And Chance wasn't improving Bowie's self-esteem. She really needed to knock him off his almighty perch. Nobody ever deserved it more.

CHANCE WASN'T PREPARED for the sight of Andi demonstrating yoga moves in the bathing suit that had made him dump coffee on his keyboard.

He tried not to watch. The sink was at right angles to the deck, and if he faced straight ahead while he washed dishes, he only caught flickers of the activity out of the corner of his eye. But, sure as the world, before long he'd be standing like an idiot, his hands motionless in the soapy water while he stared outside at Andi executing her salute to the sun.

She and Bowie faced east, which made a great deal of sense if you were saluting the sun, but that meant presenting her cute little backside to Chance, and that was not helpful, not helpful at all. Several of the moves involved bending over, which gave him a heart-stopping view of her firm and very inviting behind. When she placed both her feet and her palms on the deck and lifted her hips high in the air, he nearly broke a glass as it slipped from his fingers and clattered into the sink.

His only relief from surges of sexual arousal came from watching Bowie, who was definitely yoga-challenged. Chance didn't kid himself that he'd be any better at it than Bowie, but still, his brother's uncoordinated efforts made him chuckle. He was a little surprised that Andi didn't kid Bowie about his performance.

He regretted the exchange he'd just had with Bowie, but after the effort he put into making sure all the family investments stayed solid, it rankled to have Bowie accuse him of being preoccupied with money. As if he kept track of the stock market for his own benefit. He had little use for money, but his mother needed a strong retirement account, and Bowie needed funds for the baby's security. Everybody expected him to take care of that.

He continued to watch Andi work with Bowie, and his admiration grew. Bowie's request for a lesson had been sincere, and Andi was doing her earnest best to teach him. Good teachers didn't ridicule their students, and Andi was obviously a very good teacher. Maybe she'd finally found her niche. From what Nicole had said, Andi had been searching for the right career for years. Chance wondered if she realized just how talented an instructor she was, and if she was capitalizing on that talent.

Then, suddenly, the lesson was over, and as they turned to come back inside, Chance started washing furiously to make up for lost time.

"That was great," Bowie said. "Let's do that every morning. I've always wanted to be more flexible, and this beats ballet lessons."

"You were going to take ballet?" Chance asked. He risked looking up, and realized he shouldn't have. The exertion had left Andi's face flushed and her hair a little mussed, just as it might be if she'd been making love. God, how he ached.

"They say it's great for flexibility and rhythm, both of which I ain't got," Bowie said.

"Yoga won't be much help with rhythm," Andi said, "but you don't have a problem with that, judging from the way you danced last night."

"I've practiced a lot. Chance here picked it up naturally. Played drums in a garage band during high school."

"Really?" She gave Chance one of those looks that

fried his circuits. "I've heard drummers are the craziest members of the band."

"I was the exception." Chance returned his attention to the dishes.

"Don't believe him," Bowie said. "He had the makings of a wild man, but Dad convinced him of the error of his ways and brought him into line. I guess Dad decided I was hopeless and left me alone. Unfortunately, I had absolutely no talent for drums, so the band folded."

"I see." Andi walked over to the counter and took a dish towel off the rack. "You're not very far along on this chore, drummer boy. I'll dry."

"That's okay. You helped cook. I'll do it." The close-up scent of her brought back those heady moments from the night before, and he was having trouble breathing normally.

"I feel as if I ought to do something," she said, grabbing a dish from the strainer.

Put on more clothes, Chance thought. "I guess we should pick up everything from the beach, if we're going to leave."

"I'll do that," Bowie said. "You guys finish up the dishes." In a flash he was out the door, leaving them standing alone together at the sink.

Chance searched for something to say. He cleared his throat. "Thanks for covering for me with Nicole." He set a glass in the strainer and miraculously didn't break it in the process. His hands were shaking.

"I said I would. She may know more than she's saying, though."

"They both do." He took a deep breath and leaned both hands on the edge of the sink to steady himself. "Andi, if you have any compassion in your soul, you'll put on something extremely shapeless and ugly over that suit.''

"Bothers you, huh?''

He didn't look at her. Didn't dare. ''Yeah.''

"Bowie thinks you need to have your chain rattled.''

Chance bowed his head. ''Bowie's clueless about the kind of pressures I'm under. He has no idea what would happen to Jefferson Sporting Goods if I threw caution to the wind, like he does.''

"Or maybe he cares more about you than about that precious business.''

He stared at her.

"New concept, isn't it? Bowie watching out for you for a change. Well, drummer boy, I'm not covering up. Just remember, it's for your own good. I think I'll go check on Nicole.'' She ran a fingernail down his backbone and sauntered toward the hallway. Just before she turned the corner, she looked back at him, raised her hand to her lips and blew him a kiss.

He groaned and closed his eyes.

"That's done,'' Bowie said, coming in through the front sliding door. ''Aren't you finished with those dishes yet? You are the slowest dishwasher in the world, bro. Where's Andi?''

Under my skin. ''Checking on Nicole.''

"Good. Think I'll do the same. And by the way, you're working too hard at that dishwashing job.''

"What do you mean?''

"You've been scrubbing that same plate since I walked in the door, and it looked clean when you picked it up.'' He headed down the hallway in the same direction Andi had gone.

7

As Chance was finally rinsing the last dish, Bowie and Andi came back.

"She's got a slight backache," Bowie said. "And of course she's not supposed to take painkillers or anything. We forgot to bring the thing she uses for it, one of those gel packs you heat in the microwave. She thinks this is a stupid idea, but I'd like to go back to the marina and see if the general store has anything like that."

"Let's do it," Chance said. His pulse quickened. Oh, God, he'd have a chance to buy—no, he wouldn't think about that now. He had to concentrate on Nicole. "You're sure she's okay?"

"She seems fine," Andi said, "but those microwaveable packs are great. I recommend them to my yoga students all the time. If the general store doesn't have any, there's a little town not too far down the road. I'll volunteer to go. Then we'll have the heat pack for the whole trip. I'll bet she'd sleep better with it, too."

"Great," Bowie said. "Come on, Chance, let's get those stakes pulled up and take this sucker back in."

Chance followed his brother out to the front deck, battling his thoughts the entire time. All the reasons for not getting involved with Andi still existed. Without birth control he might be able to avoid making a stupid mistake. Not buying it would serve as a built-in brake to his runaway libido. So why was he even considering it? Because he was going insane, that's why. His famous discipline was crumbling in the face of temptation. He couldn't guarantee he wouldn't grab her in a moment of lust and say to hell with precautions. It had almost happened the night before. He wished he'd receive some sort of sign, some indication of what he should do.

"Chance?" Andi called after him.

"Yeah?" He turned around just before he was ready to leap to the sand.

"Want me to bring in the laptop?"

The laptop. It had been the furthest thing from his mind. Had it stayed balanced on the deck chair, which it would have if she hadn't reminded him, one good roll of the boat in the choppy water could have sent it into the lake. "Thanks," he said, gazing at her.

"You're welcome." She smiled at him, without a trace of sarcasm. "I know how much it means to you."

As signs went, it wasn't much. But it was a small indication that she understood the demons that plagued him, that he might, just might, be able to trust her. That when he lost his head, she might keep hers. That she wasn't trying to ambush him. Hell, he'd known all along what he wanted to do when he got to that general store. He would have taken just about anything as a sign to do it.

ALL THINGS CONSIDERED, Andi thought Chance did an admirable job of docking the houseboat. True, he brought it in a little fast and banged the prow against the dock, causing the cupboards to fly open and a few things to topple out, but nothing broke. The wind made it difficult to stay the boat's course, and he'd needed the greater speed to avoid drifting into one of the other boats as he came in.

He and Bowie headed off to the general store to try

their luck, with Nicole protesting all the while that the effort was totally unnecessary.

"Let them pamper you," Andi said as they sat on the foredeck and watched the marina activities around them. "They love it. It's not every day they get to take care of a pregnant lady."

"They do seem to be getting a kick out of this. On the plane ride out here, Chance told me about the time he and a fraternity friend helped deliver a baby when a couple got stuck in a snowstorm on the way to the hospital. I could tell it made a huge impression on him. He's pretty awed by the whole process."

"No kidding! I'm sure we'd all remember something like that. The poor woman must have been panic-stricken."

"I'm sure. I'm glad this baby will be born before the snow hits Chicago." Nicole arched her back and put her hand to the base of her spine.

"Boy, am I out of it," Andi said, getting up. "I have the perfect exercise to help you with your backache, and I haven't even shown you." She pushed aside her chair and lay down on the deck. "Come on down here beside me."

Nicole laughed. "Shouldn't we go inside and do this?"

"No, the deck floor is warmer. It'll feel good. Come on."

"You are the most uninhibited person I know. Okay, but I refuse to do that inverted vee thing where you stick your butt in the air."

"You won't have to." Andi waited until her sister was lying beside her on the deck. "Now, bring your knees up as far as your tummy will allow, and wrap your arms around them as best you can."

"Which isn't much."

"That's good enough. Now just gently rock back and forth on the small of your back, like this."

Nicole followed her directions. "Oh, Andi, that does feel good. It's like giving myself a massage."

"Told you." Andi rocked in a synchronized motion with her sister. "Close your eyes. That'll focus you on the massage and it'll feel even better."

"Oh, God, yes. That's it."

Bowie's voice came from somewhere above them. "I swear, Chance, we can't leave these women alone for a minute. Now they're in the fetal position having a religious experience on the deck."

"Don't knock it until you've tried it, Bowie Jefferson," Nicole said.

Andi opened her eyes and looked up at the two men standing over them. Bowie held a plastic bag that probably contained Nicole's gel pack. Chance had something smaller wrapped in concealing plastic clutched in his large hand. Her pulse rate picked up. The purchase she'd hoped Chance might make would come in a package about that size. She wondered if Bowie had any idea what his brother had bought at the general store.

"We were in luck, sweetheart," Bowie said. "Got just what we needed, right, Chance?"

"Right." With his aviator shades on, it was nearly impossible to read his expression, but he seemed to be looking at her. "Everybody ready to set sail?"

Andi got to her feet as Bowie helped Nicole up. Andi had the feeling Chance had been thoroughly enjoying the view of her lying on her back, knees pulled to her chest, in her revealing black suit. The game had become a little less playful and a lot more erotic. There wouldn't be burros on the beach every night. She swallowed. "Sure. Let's go for it."

ALTHOUGH ANDI campaigned for Bowie to take the boat out of the slip this time, Chance ended up at the wheel, after all. Andi told herself that she just didn't have enough leverage yet. Before the week was over, Chance would have new respect for his brother's abilities, or her name wasn't Andi Lombard.

"How about sailing down toward Hoover Dam?" she suggested as she heated the gel pack in the microwave. She'd noticed that the small package he'd had in his hand when he'd returned with Bowie had disappeared somewhere, and he'd never mentioned buying anything at the general store. Her certainty about the contents of the package grew.

"Sounds like a good idea," Bowie said. "Nic, is that okay?"

"Just fine."

"Try this on your back." Andi brought the fabric-covered gel pack to where her sister sat.

Nicole placed it at the small of her back. "Heaven. I know it was a bother to go back for this thing, but I appreciate the effort, you guys."

"Glad to do it," Chance said.

"It was important," Bowie agreed.

Andi tried to tell from their expressions if there was any double meaning to their comments. Andi had seen the general store. It wasn't large. For Chance to buy the condoms without Bowie knowing would have been difficult. Yet there were no exchanged winks or clearing of throats to indicate the brothers were giving each other invisible nudges in the ribs. If they were colluding in this effort, they were better at it than she'd have given them credit for.

The prospect that Chance would be looking for an opportunity to make love to her totally changed the way she viewed him. She became fascinated by the curve of his fingers on the wheel, the flex of his shoulders, the shift of his hips on the captain's seat, the angle of his foot. Fascinated and aroused. She hoped to hell his little package wasn't a couple of packs of chewing gum.

"Bowie, want to take the wheel for a while?" Chance asked.

"Sure," Bowie said.

"Good. I've checked my laptop, and it seems to be working okay. I'll go in the back, place some calls and make a few notes."

So his mind wasn't similarly occupied, she thought. He could plan a seduction, then efficiently continue going about his business. She was irritated that he wasn't as focused on their relationship as she was. He had a lot to learn, and she was just the woman to wake him up. "Give my regards to Wall Street," she said.

"Be glad to." He gave her a totally bland look as he turned the captain's chair over to Bowie.

Chewing gum, she thought. The jerk had probably bought himself a supply of tutti-frutti and had no intention of following through on last night's impulse. Which would save her from making the mistake of getting involved with Mr. Business-Comes-First.

Chance picked up his laptop and walked down the hallway without giving Andi another glance.

"Hey, Nic, I'll play you a game of gin," Andi said, mentally sticking out her tongue at Chance's retreating back.

Sometime later, the cards began sliding across the table of their own accord as the boat pitched from side to side. Nicole was looking a little green, and Andi turned to Bowie. "A little bumpy out there, huh, Captain?"

"Yeah." He adjusted his visor. "We talked about pulling into a sheltered cove and waiting it out if the wind picked up. What do you say we moor this tub, at least for lunch?''

"Good idea.'' Andi got a nod of approval from Nicole, who had her hand over her mouth and wasn't looking too chipper.

"I'm gonna have some of that canned chili, cut up some onions, maybe shred some cheese,'' Bowie said. "How does that sound, Nic, honey?'' He looked over at her. "A little woozy, babe?''

Nicole nodded.

He smiled. "Then you don't have to fix my chili.''

"I just may fix your chili, buddy-boy.'' Andi scowled at him as she stood and gazed at the shoreline. "Hey, up ahead, see that spot with outcroppings on both sides of the beach? We'll slip in there, tie up and be protected from the wind. Are you ready for that, sis?''

Nicole nodded again.

"Okay, I'll take us over there.'' Bowie eased the boat to the right. "Man, can you feel the boat hydroplaning?''

Andi walked over to put a hand on his shoulder. "Maybe it's time to have a silent cockpit.'' She rolled her eyes in Nicole's direction. "Want me to go get Chance?''

"If I know him, he's on his way down the hall.''

"We're bobbing around like a damn cork,'' Chance said as he walked into the room.

"What'd I tell you?'' Bowie said under his breath.

"Good thing we don't have anybody who gets seasick in this group,'' Chance said, setting his laptop on the table. "Rocking back and forth like this would sure bring on the upchucks if we did.''

Nicole bolted from her seat and rushed past him toward the bathroom.

He stared after her. "What's the matter with Nicole?"

"Way to go, Einstein," Andi said as she started down the hall.

"God, I'm sorry. I had no idea." Chance sounded contrite.

"Nic hates people to pay attention to her when she gets like this," Bowie called after Andi.

"I know," Andi said, but she continued anyway. "Nic?" She tapped on the door. "Let me help you, hon."

"I'm okay," came a muffled response.

Andi stood there, unsure how much to push. Bowie was right—Nicole hated having anyone see her in embarrassing circumstances. "I'll check back in a minute," Andi said finally.

By the time she returned, Bowie was heading the boat into the inlet. Jagged, narrow rock walls rose on either side.

"Not much maneuverability in here," Chance said.

"Yeah, but the rock walls on either side will protect us from the wind," Bowie said.

"Still, I'm not—"

"No use debating. We have to moor," Andi said. "Nicole needs to get off this boat for a little while and let her stomach settle down."

"You're right." Chance stood behind Bowie. "Looks like there's a channel there we can use to get in. There's not a whole lot of clearance, but we can make it."

"Andi," Bowie said, "go back to the bathroom and warn Nic when we're ready to hit the beach. I don't want her losing any teeth."

"Okay." Andi started toward the bathroom.

"And brace yourself," Chance said. "With this much wind, we need to really dig into that sand."

"Right." She looked into his eyes and drew comfort

from the confidence she saw there. A little wind on the lake wasn't going to panic a man like Chance Jefferson. She held on to that thought as she went to the bathroom door. "Nic? Hold on, kid. We're going up on the beach, and we're going in fast and hard."

"Okay," came the weak response.

"Want me in there with you?"

"Nope."

"Here we go," called Chance from the front of the boat.

Andi grabbed the doorjamb and flexed her knees. Whomp! She nearly lost her grip as the force of the impact threw her forward. She recovered herself and pressed her ear to the bathroom door. "Nic?"

The door opened, and a pale Nicole stood patting a washcloth over her face. "Good thing you warned me," she said with a little smile. "Otherwise I would have beaned myself on the toilet lid, and Lord knows how I would have explained that to my mother-in-law. She was very much against my coming on this trip. She thought Bowie and Chance should go alone. Which made me all the more determined to be here, of course."

"Of course. That's the Lombard spirit coming through. And the meddling battle-ax will never have to hear a thing about this." Andi put her arm around Nicole. "How about a glass of water?"

"Fine."

Andi walked her slowly into the kitchen, got her the water and waited while she sipped it.

"Ready to get off this tub for a while?"

"Sure."

As they walked to the front of the boat, the ringing sound of sledgehammers against iron stakes told Andi that the brothers were already mooring the boat.

"Oooh, Bowie, let's rent a houseboat," Nicole said, mimicking herself. "It'll be so cool. We'll lie around in the sun, fish, and feel the gentle rock of the waves. Ha."

"We did that yesterday," Andi said, giving her a hug. "You wanted two days of that? Greedy woman."

"I'm sorry I barfed, Andi. How gross."

"I'm sorry, too, but only for your sake." She walked Nicole out on deck. "Nobody minds. Are you okay?"

"Feeling better every minute. But I can hardly wait to put my feet on solid ground."

"Solid ground, coming up." Andi called to the men, who immediately came over and helped Nicole to the sand. Andi handed down chairs and towels so they could establish a little camp.

"Are you coming down?" Nicole asked.

"In a minute. I'll rustle up some beer and chips for our gallant lads first. Want anything?"

Nicole swallowed. "Not yet."

"I'll be there in a minute." Andi walked inside and almost tripped over Chance's laptop lying on the floor. She stooped to pick it up from where it had apparently fallen when the boat hit the beach. He must have been so concerned about getting the boat firmly anchored and Nicole on steady footing that he hadn't even noticed.

As much as she resented the darn thing, she didn't want it to be broken and all the information in it lost. She set it on the table and snapped it open. Everything looked fine, but she'd been around computers enough to know that looks were deceiving. The thing could be deader than a doornail. She flipped the switch and the screen began to glow. So far, so good.

The operating program came up, but that didn't always mean anything, either. She clicked the mouse and opened his list of files. If one of the files opened okay, then the laptop was probably okay. She glanced over the cryptic list and picked one with the initials AL, just for the heck of it. She expected a report on Athletes and Litigation, or Assets and Liabilities. Chance wouldn't have a file on her in his precious laptop, for heaven's sake.

But he did.

Andi gasped, and then her eyes narrowed. Oh, he would pay for this. Nobody listed the pros and cons of making love to her on some *spreadsheet* and got away with it. He made an emotional choice sound like some sort of corporate decision.

Andi skimmed down the pro side and read sentences like: *She excites me more than any woman I've known* and *Touching her would give me intense pleasure.* Now, that was sort of nice, even listed coldly in columns. It made her tingle. A lot. But there were less complimentary phrases on the con side such as: *She'll destroy my concentration* and *Her wacky view of life spells trouble.*

"Oh, I'm going to spell trouble, all right. And you won't need a spell-checker to know when it's arrived," she muttered. After typing *Who cares?* next to the sentence about destroying concentration, she highlighted the *wacky view* sentence and switched it to the pro side. Then she changed *wacky* to *unique* and *spells trouble* to *fascinates me.*

Apparently Chance was confused. He'd written, *Her kiss blots out all reason* in both columns. Andi deleted it from the con side. Kisses were *supposed* to blot out all reason. Otherwise there was no point in kissing. Boy, did he have a lot to learn. For good measure, she added another sentence to the pro side. *She's the most beautiful woman I've ever known* looked very nice on the screen. It looked so good, she added another: *Her intelligence is matched by her sweetness and charm.*

"Hey, Andi!" Bowie called from the beach. "Are you brewing the beer yourself?"

She jumped. "Be right there!" She'd forgotten all about her errand. Quickly she saved the information on the screen, closed the file and turned off the computer.

As she pulled beer from the refrigerator, she considered what Chance would do when he opened the file and discovered her changes. Then she smiled. He wouldn't be likely to make a public scene, now, would he? She had him. And at least she knew he'd been writing about her instead of doing his work. That almost made up for his stupidity in thinking that she could be reduced to a list on a computer screen.

CHANCE DIDN'T LIKE the quality of the sand holding the mooring stakes. The night before there had been a more solid feel to the way the stakes went into the ground, and he'd never doubted they'd hold, even in a wind. The sand was more loosely packed here, but they had to do the best they could to secure the boat. Even if Nicole wasn't seasick, he couldn't imagine how they'd back out of this narrow spot with the wind blowing the way it was. He would have preferred a different mooring inlet, but this was the one they had, and they'd make the best of it. To anchor the stakes more securely, he and Bowie piled large rocks around them.

They decided to have a picnic on the beach. Although gusts of wind blew sand into their food during the meal, nobody suggested going back on the boat. At least two-thirds of the hull remained in the water, and there was too much motion to consider moving the picnic inside and risking a relapse for Nicole. Chance kept an eye on the stakes, which seemed to be holding.

After lunch, Bowie and Nicole walked to the edge of

the water to rinse the dishes. Chance pretended to doze on a beach towel, but he soon became completely absorbed watching Andi throw potato chips to a pair of ravens. Bigger and glossier than the crows he'd seen in the Midwest, they would glide down from the rock ledges where they apparently lived, seize the morsels she threw and retreat again.

Andi's blond hair danced and became tangled in the wind, making her look like a wild thing herself as she called to the birds, coaxing them nearer. His eyes hidden behind shades, he was able to study the lace-covered strips of bare skin revealed by her black suit, and how the lace shifted as she leaned down to get more chips and toss them gracefully to the birds.

He allowed himself to imagine kissing his way down those lace strips before he slowly peeled them away. Much as he loved his brother and sister-in-law, he wished they could beam themselves somewhere else for about two hours. Knowing they'd trudge back up the beach any minute, he turned over on his stomach to hide the evidence of his thoughts. The warm sand shifted a little beneath his erection, but it wasn't nearly the sensation he had in mind.

The potato-chip bag was within reach. He pulled it over just as Andi turned and came back for more chips.

She walked toward him and dropped to her knees in front of him. "You have my chips."

He propped his head on one hand and looked up at her. "Want some?"

She held out her hand.

He reached into the bag, took out one chip and put it in her outstretched hand.

Her gray-green eyes were covered by sunglasses, but

the corners of her full mouth tilted up. "You're flirting with me, right?"

"Right."

"So, did you go shopping this morning, too?" she asked.

"Would it make any difference to you if I did?"

"Possibly."

"Then it's possible I went shopping."

"Oh my God!" Bowie shouted. "Chance! The stakes!"

Chance surged to his feet at the sound of Bowie's shout. One set of stakes had pulled out, and the huge boat was blowing sideways. If somebody didn't turn the craft, it would wedge itself on the beach, the motors out of the water. They'd be marooned.

8

CHANCE SPLASHED into the water and grabbed the mooring stakes just as Bowie leaped in beside him and took hold of the ropes. Pulling together they battled the wind that pushed relentlessly against the side of the houseboat.

Andi joined them, latching on to a section of rope. "Problem?"

"Hell, no," Chance said. "We're just showing off."

"Glad to hear it. I hate problems." She started pulling with him.

Nicole appeared beside Bowie and put her hands on the taut rope.

"No, Nicole!" Bowie said, his voice a stern command.

"But—"

"You might hurt yourself. No."

Chance had never heard his usually laid-back brother take such charge of a situation. He was impressed. "Nic, go stand on the beach and guide us," he said, breathing heavily. "Andi, climb in the boat and turn on the motors. If we get it headed in straight again, gun it." He prayed this highly independent woman wouldn't question him.

She didn't. "Right." She started running toward the prow of the boat. Then she turned. "What if the stakes on the other side pull out, too?"

Chance managed a grim smile. "Don't leave without us."

"Right." She took off.

Bowie strained at the ropes. "Maybe we'll rent something a little smaller next time?"

Chance gritted his teeth and planted his feet. His arms began to ache. "A canoe."

"A boogie board."

Chance snorted. "Nic, are we moving it at all?"

"A little."

The engines roared to life.

"Now," Bowie said, "if we can just pull it around so it's straight, Andi can ram it back up on the beach."

"Yep." Chance gasped for breath as he renewed his efforts. Unfortunately the wind seemed to do the same, blowing harder than ever. "Just straighten it out. No problem."

Bowie pulled until the muscles bulged in his arms, but he staggered farther into the water as the boat continued to swing in the wrong direction. "Anytime, Chance."

"I was waiting for you." Chance felt the water lick the bottom of his shorts, and the sandy bottom had given way to slippery rocks. "Didn't want to show you up in front of Nicole."

"You're losing ground!" Nicole called.

"You know, I didn't notice," Bowie muttered breathlessly to Chance. He stood up to his waist in water. "Did you notice?"

"I can't get my footing on these damn rocks." *Rocks.* "Nic, how much clearance does Andi have for the propellers?" he yelled.

"I'll see!"

Almost immediately came the sound of giant ice cubes being crushed in a blender the size of...the houseboat. Then the motors stopped.

"Not much clearance," Nicole said. "In fact, I think she hit 'em."

Chance gazed at Bowie. "Gee, do you think?"

"Could be. Plus, my shoulder's about to be dislocated."

"Mine, too," Chance said tightly.

"Ever moved a houseboat that's stuck sideways on the beach?"

"Bet it would be easier once the wind's died down."

"Let 'er go, Chance. This houseboat's bigger than both of us."

"This houseboat's bigger than Detroit."

"We're letting go!" Bowie called to Andi and Nicole. "The boat will just drift sideways up on the beach."

"Won't that be a problem?" Nicole called back.

"Nothing we can't handle!" Chance shouted.

Bowie laughed. "And if they believe that, we've been playing our cards way too close to our chest."

"On three," Chance said. "One, two, *three*."

The brothers released the stakes and ropes. Slowly the boat turned until it was broadside to the buffeting wind. Then it edged toward the shore until the side crunched into the sand. Wedged tight.

Once the inevitable had happened, the adrenaline rush subsided and Chance had time for remorse. "This is my fault," he said as they waded out of the water. "I knew the sand wasn't stable enough. I should have paid more attention."

"I knew it wasn't stable, too. Why isn't it my fault?"

"Because I'm—"

"Older? Wiser? The biggest martyr the world has ever known? Come on, look on the bright side," Bowie said. "From this angle we'll be able to get a premiere view of those completely uninsured propellers."

Chance grimaced. "Don't remind me. That's the other

thing I should have thought of. I knew we didn't have much clearance.''

"Oh, lighten up. Stuff happens.''

"That's pretty much your attitude about life, isn't it? I hate to think what would happen if I started thinking like that.''

"You *might* start acting like a normal human being instead of a superhero.''

Chance's jaw tightened. "I can't afford mistakes.''

"I'll tell you what you can't afford, man.'' Bowie paused to face him. "You can't afford this need to be perfect.''

"I don't need to be perfect!''

"The hell you don't! You're so petrified of making a mistake that you work night and day, supposedly for the good of the ones you care about. But what kind of caring is that, when you never spend any time with us because you're so damn busy?'' A flush spread across Bowie's face and he looked away. But he didn't retract a word.

Chance stared at him, his heart thudding painfully in his chest. "That's what you used to say about Dad.''

"Yeah, well, he would have been real proud of you. You've turned out just like he expected. And so have I.'' Bowie glanced at him. "For a minute there, when we were working together to get this boat straightened out, I had the feeling we were a team. We'd worked as a team to screw things up, and we'd take the blame together and try to work it out together. But apparently you want all the blame, and when the time comes, all the glory. Well, take it away, bro. It's all yours.'' He continued toward the beach.

ANDI COULD HEAR Chance and Bowie arguing as they came out of the water together. This was no time for dissension in the ranks. She walked out on the deck. "Hey, guys!"

They both looked up at her.

"Is it time to use Chance's cell phone to call the Coast Guard?"

"The *Coast Guard?*" Bowie said.

"Yeah. Somebody who knows something about getting boats unstuck."

Bowie turned to Chance, as if waiting for whatever command would come next.

Chance cleared his throat. "We let it get stuck on purpose," he said. "That was the plan."

Bowie stared at him for a few seconds. "Exactly," he said at last. "For a windbreak. You women need some protection from the wind."

"I see." She glanced at Nicole, who'd walked down to meet the guys. "They say they did this on purpose, for a windbreak."

Nicole looked doubtful. "Really."

Andi folded her arms. "And how did you two geniuses plan to get us unstuck again, wait for the tide to come in?"

"Well, we—" Bowie turned to Chance. "Tell the women the plan, Chance."

"Why don't you tell it?" Chance said, gazing at his brother.

"Okay. We, uh, we figured when the wind dies down, we can pull on the ropes from one side, and push from the other side, and—"

"I'm calling 911," Andi said. "You two don't have a clue, but like typical males, you'd rather sit here forever wedged into the sand than ask for backup and look stupid." She turned around.

"Wait!" Chance called. "Let's not rush into this."

"Do they even have a Coast Guard station around here?" Bowie asked Chance in a tone so low Andi almost missed the comment.

She turned back in time to see Chance shrug. Clueless, both of them. "How long do you want me to wait?" she asked.

"Just a little while," Chance said. "See if the wind dies down. I'm sure Bowie and I can use leverage on this puppy as long as we're not fighting the wind."

"What about the propellers?" Nicole asked.

Bowie clasped his hands in front of him. "Well, by golly, we were just on our way to take a look, weren't we, Chance?"

"We were, as a matter of fact."

"Before you head around that way, would one of you gentlemen help me down?" Andi asked. "There seems to be a lake where the sand used to be."

"Oh. Right." Chance turned toward Bowie and Nicole. "You guys go ahead. We'll be along."

Chance waded out to the back of the boat. "Just hold on to my shoulders and I'll lift you down."

"Are you and Bowie having a problem?" she asked in a low voice.

"Nothing that a miracle couldn't fix."

"Chance—"

"Never mind. Bowie's had his say and I have some thinking to do. Come on down and we'll go see what shape the propeller's in."

She got to her knees at the opening in the railing and followed his directions. Touching his smooth, sweat-dampened skin started to blur her thinking, right when she needed to keep her mind clear to evaluate the situation.

"That's it. Just lean into me," he said. He reached up and placed his hands firmly around her waist.

If touching him was disorienting, having him touch her was worse, setting loose disturbing little tremors throughout her body. "I think we need to call for help, Chance," she said. "I think that would be the wise thing to do."

"You may be right, but I'd like to avoid it if we can." He started lifting her down.

"To preserve your pride? Because—"

"It's a little more complicated than that."

"Well, I just want you to know that I—" She lost her place in the sentence as he eased her down, causing her to slide against him in the process.

"That you what?" He set her gently into the shallow water, but he didn't take his hands from her waist.

She looked up at him. For some reason her hands still rested on his shoulders, and she was reluctant to move them. In fact, she'd begun unconsciously kneading the muscles beneath her fingers, and her heartbeat just kept getting faster. "That I..."

He reached up to take off his sunglasses. "Yeah, me, too," he murmured as he lowered his head.

Her eyes drifted closed as he took unquestioning possession of her mouth. She was lost. If she ever wrote out a pros and cons list for Chance, the pro side would have several entries about his kiss. She'd list how he managed to exert the most exquisite pressure, urgent but never bruising, that brought about her complete surrender. As he wrapped his arms tightly around her, she molded herself to him with a soft moan of pleasure.

He lifted his mouth a fraction from hers, but he continued to hold her very close. "I don't want anybody towing us out of this cove and back to the marina if we can help it," he said softly as his lips brushed hers. "For several reasons. This is just one of them."

She had trouble getting her breath. "I'm beginning…to understand."

"Good." He deepened the kiss, and his tongue boldly claimed her in a way that left no doubt as to his intentions. Then he slowly released her. "But no matter what I want or don't want," he said, his voice husky, "we have to find out how Nicole's doing and make a decision based on that."

She took a long, steadying breath. "Of course."

"If she's not feeling well, then we'll call for help and if necessary, get towed out of here and back to the marina."

"Right."

"But if she's feeling okay, we'll get the boat unstuck when the wind dies down, which might not be until morning." His gaze moved over her, as if he was anticipating what might happen between them before dawn.

"Yes."

Passion flared in his eyes. Then he put his sunglasses back on. "Let's go look at those propellers and talk to Nicole."

She gazed up at him in dreamy contentment. "I'm sure at least one set is mangled beyond belief."

"I'm sure you're right." He smiled down at her. "Funny, but I don't seem to give a damn."

THAT WAS A GOOD THING, Andi thought a little later as she looked at the mess that she'd help create by running the motors as the boat swung into a bed of rocks.

"I'm guessing what we have now," Bowie said, "is a single screw."

"On a boat designed for a twin-screw," Chance added, wading out in the water to examine the bent propeller. "But airplanes can fly with an engine out, so I'm sure this boat can do fine, once it's not battling a killer wind.'' He turned to Nicole. "But there are no guarantees. How are you feeling, Nicole?''

"Fine, now that I'm not rocking and rolling on that boat.''

"The wind might keep up until tomorrow, and we'd be stuck on this beach until then. If we call somebody now, we can get towed out of here.''

"Towed?" Bowie grimaced. "Aw, Chance.''

Nicole smiled at her husband. "Poor manly man. Don't worry, sweetheart. As long as it's still windy, I have no desire to get on the boat, whether we're under our own steam or being towed. In fact, if it's windy for the rest of the week, this might be right where I'd vote to stay.''

"Then I guess—'' Chance paused and glanced at Bowie. "What do you think?''

"I think we should wait for the wind to die down and see what we can do with this barn. We have plenty of supplies, so that's not a problem.''

Chance turned to Andi. "What's your vote?''

"If Nicole wants to stay, that's fine with me.''

"Then it's settled,'' Chance said. "Anybody for a swim?''

"You all go ahead,'' Nicole said. "I want to park a deck chair in the shade of this windbreak you've created and read a romance novel.''

"I'll sit beside you and feed you grapes,'' Bowie said, putting his arm around her.

"You just want to read the juicy parts over my shoulder,'' Nicole said.

Andi could see where this was heading. The couples were dividing up. Then she remembered she had yet to see Chance in a bathing suit. "I'll swim with you,'' she said.

"Great." He waded out of the water and headed toward the back of the boat. "I'll go put on my suit."

Andi thought offering to help him might be a little obvious. "Toss down a few deck chairs and we'll get Nicole set up. She needs an extra one for her feet, too."

"Sure." Chance heaved himself out of the shallow water and onto the deck.

"Oh, and maybe you should warm up that microwave thing for her back," Bowie said. "And her book's on the shelf above our bed, if you could get that, too."

"Hey, guys," Nicole said. "Don't treat me like an invalid. I barfed. I had a slight backache. No big deal. I came on this trip to have fun with all of you and enjoy my last few weeks of freedom, but I didn't come to be fussed over."

Chance leaned over the railing and smiled down at her. "In that case, would you mind straightening this boat out? It seems to be stuck and none of us can do a damn thing about it."

"And after that, you can give me a rubdown and a beer," Bowie said.

"And gather firewood and rocks for a fire circle," Andi added. "Oh, and if you could—"

"Hey, all right! I get the point! Fussing's good. I like fussing."

"That's better," Chance said. "Deck chairs, coming down."

Nicole glanced up at him. "And a bowl of ice cream?"

"Okay."

"With some of that fudge sauce Andi brought?"

"You're sure you don't want me to whip up some baked Alaska? I'll be in the kitchen anyway."

Nicole smiled sweetly at him. "Not right this minute. I'll let you know."

After Chance passed down the deck chairs, along with a cooler full of beer and Nicole's gel pack, book and ice cream, he disappeared inside to change into his suit. As Nicole exclaimed over the wonders of Andi's fudge sauce, Bowie came over and gave Andi a smacking kiss on the cheek.

"What was that for?" she asked.

"Whatever you said to Chance while he was helping you off the boat."

"Believe me, I didn't say anything."

"Okay, then, whatever you did. And I'm not asking. But it's had a good effect, whatever it was. He actually asked for our opinions for a change."

Andi blushed. "Maybe he's finally starting to get the message that he's not God."

"Looks like. He even condescended to go swimming."

Nicole looked up from her bowl of ice cream. "You have to remember, though, that he may well slip right back into his old ways after this trip."

"Yeah, that's true," Bowie said. "But it's a start. And I think Andi's been a good influence."

"Now *that* would be a first," Andi said. Then her attention was thoroughly captured by the man who walked out on deck in sexy black trunks. "Last one in is a rotten egg," she called to him, and without seeing whether he'd heard her or not, she ran down to the water.

Splashing her way around the end of the boat until she was waist-deep in the lake, she looked up just in time to see Chance execute a shallow dive off the side and disappear under the surface. The wind ruffled the water, making it impossible for her to see beneath it.

Launching herself into the coolness, she swam to the area where she'd seen him disappear. Fear clutched at her stomach at the thought that he might have hit his head on a submerged rock. Men were so foolish. They always had to do one of those macho dives when they had no idea what was under the waves.

A hand closed around her ankle, and a moment later she was under the water, in his arms. Holding her tight, he kicked to the surface and grabbed one of the loose mooring ropes that dangled from the lake side of the boat.

"You scared me," she said, gasping. "You shouldn't be diving into water you can't see under."

"That was the channel we came in through." He worked his way up the rope so they drew nearer the boat and shallow water. "I knew it was okay."

"Then why did you have to stay under and scare me like that?"

"It's part of the coed swimming game," he said, grinning at her. "You say, 'Last one in's a rotten egg,' which is me, so I have to get back by grabbing you from under the water. I thought you said you went to junior high?"

"I did, but it's hard to picture you there."

"Oh, I was there. That's where I learned to take off a bra with one flick of my fingers." His chest muscles flexed, creating a sensuous friction against her breasts as he eased along the length of the rope.

His nearness and the conversation were heating her up, and fast. "Tell me," she asked. "Do guys steal their sister's bras and practice that technique by fastening them around the back of a chair?"

"Maybe, but I didn't have a sister, so I had to practice on the real thing."

"Gee, that must have been tough."

"Sheer hell." He let go of the rope when they were within a short distance of the boat. "Can your feet touch here?"

She wiggled her toes toward the bottom. "No."

"That's okay. I can. Wrap your legs around me, Andi."

She did, and immediately realized how aroused he was. Glancing up into his fevered gaze, made even more intense by the moisture spiking his dark lashes, she decided there was nothing sexier than a gray-flannel-suit type who was, even temporarily, unplugged. As her attention drifted to his mouth, she noticed the glistening drop clinging to his full lower lip. She slowly wiped it away. "Aren't we going to swim?" she murmured.

"Not if I can help it."

9

THE PRIVACY CREATED by the shelter of the boat made Andi bold. "Then I guess you'd better kiss me."

Chance smiled. "Where?"

She placed a finger against her lips. "You can start here."

And start he did, with an inborn talent that soon had the blood pounding through her veins.

After several seconds he drew back very slowly. "Where else?" he murmured in a husky voice.

Mouth tingling, her whole body coursing with need, she leaned back in his arms and tilted her head as she traced a circle on her exposed throat. "Here."

He licked and nibbled as she ran her finger along her shoulder. Taking her bathing-suit strap in his teeth, he pulled it down before nuzzling her shoulder. "Now where?"

Andi slipped her arm out of the strap and cradled her breast just above the cool lap of the water. "Here."

"Devil woman." He eased down into the water and took her nipple into his mouth.

Fierce desire tightened the womanly core deep within her as he suckled and licked. Whimpering softly, she wrapped her legs closer around him, pressing herself against his erection. She was going slowly crazy. "Stop," she whispered, easing away from the delicious feel of his mouth on her breast. "I can't take this. Now without being able to..."

He cupped her face in one hand and pressed his lips gently over her damp face. "I can help you if you'll loosen up."

"That's the problem. I'm so loose all I can think of is having you make love to me."

"Which I want to do." He slid his hand down to her inner thigh. "I meant loosen up here."

She held his gaze and relaxed the grip of her thighs around his torso. The elastic of her suit gave way before the questing probe of his fingers. As he found the pulse that was throbbing so desperately for release, she gasped.

"There?" he murmured.

She could barely breathe. "Yes."

His voice was a low rumble of restrained desire as he stroked her. "I would kiss you there, too, but I might drown."

She closed her eyes, transported on a wave of pleasure. "Who...cares?"

The next thing she knew, he'd slid beneath the water, pulled the fabric aside and pressed his mouth against her flash point. She wriggled free and sank down to take him firmly by the shoulders. As she urged him to the surface, he brought her up with him and they clung together, breathing hard.

"I was kidding," she said, gasping. "I don't want you to drown."

His chest heaved as he drew in several gulps of air. "Some things are worth drowning for. I would have died a happy man."

She wound her arms around his neck. "You're absolutely insane."

"And it's your fault." He kissed her again, thrusting his tongue deep until she moaned in frustration.

He lifted his lips from hers a fraction. "Let's try something." He turned her slowly in the water until her back was to him and the water sloshed just above her collarbone. Then he pulled her in tight with one hand around her waist. "That's better." He nuzzled her neck as he pushed the other strap down. "Lean into me, Andi. It feels so good when you do."

She hooked her feet behind his knees and locked herself against his arousal. "Somebody's a little worked up," she murmured.

"Somebody's a lot worked up," he said, his mouth close to her ear. "It's a small price I pay for touching you like this." Beneath the concealing water he pushed her suit to her waist and cupped her breast in his hand, stroking his thumb across her nipple until she quivered in his embrace. He leaned close to her ear. "I've wanted to strip this suit off from the first minute I saw you in it."

Her breathing was ragged. "Is that why you spilled your coffee?"

"Yes, that's why I spilled my coffee." He nipped her earlobe. "And then you just had to go out on the deck and wave that tempting bottom of yours in the air, didn't you? Did you know how I'd react?"

"I had hopes."

"You've been driving me crazy all day. You're the reason I wasn't paying attention when the stakes pulled out, and why I'm here right now, loving you instead of making calls and writing memos."

She leaned her head against his strong shoulder and arched into his touch. "Good."

"Yes, it is," he murmured against her ear. "And it's about to get better." He shifted his hold, wrapping his arm beneath her breasts as he slipped his free hand inside the front panel of her suit.

She drew in her breath as he teased his way down through her wet curls and pushed into the moist channel that ached for him.

"Better?" he whispered, stroking her.

"Mmm." She shuddered as the tension began to build to an almost unbearable level.

"It's risky," he said into her ear. "If you cry out, we might have company."

As he lightly caressed the nub of her passion, holding her on a maddening plateau of desire, all she wanted was release, whatever the cost. "I...won't. Please, Chance."

His touch grew firmer and more rhythmic as he held her tight against his body.

So close. So very close. She whimpered and pressed the back of her hand to her mouth.

"Shh. Now." He pushed deep and pressed upward.

Her world exploded, and she rammed her fist into her mouth to stop the cry that rose from her throat as she convulsed in his strong grip.

He turned her around and gathered her close, kissing her face, her hair, her throat as she clung to him limply and tried to catch her breath. Gently he repositioned the straps of her suit.

As her sanity slowly returned, she gave him a long, sensuous kiss. Then she eased away from him, held up both arms and slipped under the cool water. She allowed herself to sink until she was even with his hips. Figuring he needed a surprise as well as some pleasure, she hooked her thumbs in his suit and pulled it down in one lightning move that freed his manhood. She had a split second to admire his impressive dimensions before he hauled her to the surface.

"And what are you doing, devil woman?" he asked, crushing her against him.

"I figured I could die happy."

"I'm not letting you drown, either."

"But I'll bet you'll let me do this." She reached down and grasped his shaft firmly.

He gasped. "I...might."

She stroked him, paying special attention to the sensitive tip, as she gazed into his eyes.

The blue of his irises grew dark and a muscle tensed in his jaw.

"This is risky," she murmured. "If you cry out, we might have company."

He said nothing, but his breathing quickened.

"Ah, no promises from you, I see. No begging, either. I'll bet I could make you beg, but as mellow as I'm feeling, I won't." She caressed him deliberately, relentlessly, as he trembled and grabbed at the rope to steady himself.

At last he shuddered, wrapped both arms around her and pulled her down under the water, where they melded together in a slow-motion dance until he captured her mouth in a gentle kiss as they drifted slowly back to the surface. All this unbelievable pleasure, she thought, and they hadn't even made it to the main event. She was beginning to wonder if by tempting the likes of Chauncey M. Jefferson the Fourth, she'd bitten off more than she could chew.

CHANCE HAD HOPED the interlude in the water would give him some relief from his obsession with Andi, but no such luck. After they returned to the beach, she pulled up a deck chair next to Nicole's and they started reading sexy passages aloud from Nicole's novel. Chance joined Bowie in the bawdy discussion that followed each reading, but beneath his lighthearted laughter desire boiled and flowed like lava.

Behind the protection of his sunglasses, he followed Andi's every gesture, traced the contours of her laughing mouth, focused on the curve of her breast and the tilt of her thigh. Although it was obvious Andi and Nicole had shared books like this aloud before, Chance figured Andi had initiated the activity now just to taunt him and keep him at a fever pitch. If total conquest was her goal, she was waging one helluva campaign.

"How are real guys supposed to compete with the heroes of those books?" Bowie asked.

"Sweetheart, you stack up just fine against them," Nicole said.

He adjusted his visor. "Well, I knew that. But I meant ordinary guys, like Chance, here."

"It's a struggle." Chance looked at Andi. "The dragons just aren't out there waiting to be slain like they used to be."

"That's what you think," Andi said.

"So you have dragons that need slaying, lady?"

She gave him a little smile. "Every day."

"Tell me about it," Nicole said. "There's the dragon of the leaking brake line, and the dragon of the frayed lamp cord, and the dragon of the tight jar lid, and the dragon of the plain old blues."

Bowie raised his fist. "And I slew them, every one."

"My hero." Nicole smiled at him.

The exchange had the most curious effect on Chance. He longed to play the same role for a woman, a woman like…Andi. The only times he could claim to be a hero on a white horse involved Jefferson Sporting Goods. And a company couldn't smile at you with love the way Nicole was smiling at Bowie. He was—hard as it was to believe—jealous of Bowie's life.

The sun was beginning to sink behind the mountains, and he wished he had the power to personally shove it below the horizon. He wanted the cover of night so he could be alone with Andi again, alone to make love and to explore the unusual feelings this vacation had offered him.

"Well, this hero is ready to eat dinner," Bowie said. "Time to form our little supply line again, build a fire, all that hero stuff. Ready, Chance?"

Chance sent Andi a look. "Yes."

ANDI WAS WORRIED about Nicole. She didn't think either of the men had noticed, but Nicole was in pain. Maybe only another woman would notice the little hitch in her laughter, or the way she twisted in her seat and pressed her hand low on her belly when she thought nobody was watching. Andi was watching.

As the men gathered rocks and driftwood to build a fire, Andi leaned toward Nicole. "What is it?"

"What's what?"

"Don't pretend with me. Something's bothering you."

"It's nothing. Just little...twinges."

"The baby?"

Nicole chuckled. "Yeah. She probably wants to join the discussion."

"In French."

"Right."

"How long have these twinges been going on?"

"Not long." Nicole put her hand on Andi's arm. "Please don't make a big deal of it. I've talked to lots of women who've had babies, and you get all sorts of things like this. Nothing to worry about."

"Not if you're sitting at home, right next to a phone and blocks from a hospital. This is a little different. The houseboat's not even sailable right now, and even if it were, it doesn't have running lights. The manual says very plainly not to go out on the lake at night with it."

"I don't need to go anywhere." Nicole's grip tightened on Andi's arm. "This has been so good for me, Andi. I'm not letting anything spoil it."

"But—"

"Bowie's great, but I've missed being with you, especially at a time like this. And I can't tell you how grateful I am that he and Chance are talking again."

"Even if it leads to arguments?"

"Arguments are better than no discussion at all. Chance was well on his way to being just like his father, but I see signs that he could still be saved."

"Such as?"

"Take a look." Nicole glanced over toward the cliffs.

Andi watched as the brothers dueled with sticks. Chance's stick kept breaking, until he was dueling with a piece about five inches long. As he continued to thrust and parry, laughing all the while, the setting sun gave his skin a ruddy glow, and he looked very hero-like indeed. A telltale emotion twisted her heart. It felt like...no. She didn't want to start building castles in the sky.

"I'd be in heaven if those two became friends again," Nicole said.

Andi glanced at her. "That's all well and good, but you have to promise to tell me if the twinges get worse. We have Chance's cell phone. We'll do something."

Nicole patted her arm. "That isn't going to be necessary. Besides, you know how I hate drama like that, especially if I'm in the middle of it."

AN HOUR LATER, shortly after dinner, Andi was wondering how long before she and Chance could steal off into the shadows for some serious necking, when Nicole cried out.

They all rushed to her side.

"I think I'd better...go back to the boat," she said. "I—oh, dammit!" She doubled over.

"You're in labor!" Andi cried.

Nicole lifted her face, her expression defiant. "I am *not*. It's just gas. I'll be—*augh!*"

Bowie squatted in front of her. "If that's gas, we're gonna have to give you an antacid the size of a manhole cover."

"Don't make me laugh. It hurts."

Chance gazed at her. "Childbirth does, I hear."

"Childbirth?" Bowie sounded frantic. "But it's only seven months! The baby's not done yet!"

"It's...a little more than seven months," Nicole said.

Bowie stared at her. "You were pregnant before the wedding?"

"A little."

Andi gasped. "Omigod. How pregnant?"

"Six weeks."

"And you didn't tell me?" Bowie shouted.

"I didn't want your mother to know!"

"I wouldn't have told my friggin' mother!"

"I wasn't sure!"

"Oh, Nic," Andi said, her heart aching that her sister hadn't felt free to confide in her. "You could have told me."

Nicole looked miserable. "I was afraid to tell anyone. I didn't want anything to spoil the wedding...or this vacation."

"But your doctor," Andi said. "Surely she knew. I can't believe she let you come on—"

"I didn't exactly tell her about it."

"Nic!" Bowie yelled, his face red.

"I had to be here! We all did! And first babies are supposed to be late!"

Chance drew a deep breath. "None of this matters now, guys. The main thing is to get her inside."

"You're right," Andi said, drawing strength from his calm voice. "Let's go."

As the men helped Nicole to her feet, fluid rushed down her bare legs.

"Oh my God," Bowie said. "Now she's leaking."

"It's okay, Bowie," Chance said, his voice amazingly gentle. "That's part of it. She'll be fine."

"Easy for you to say." Nicole doubled over with another pain.

"Aw, geez," Bowie said. "We didn't finish that birthing class, either."

"You're about to get a crash course," Chance said. "Let's go."

It took all three of them to lift Nicole, who kept convulsing with pain, up to the deck of the houseboat, but they eventually accomplished it.

"My bed," Chance said. "Hold her right there and I'll open it up."

Andi and Bowie supported Nicole until Chance returned. Nicole looked pale, but Bowie looked white as the plastic deck chairs.

"Bowie and I will get her into bed," Chance said to Andi. "My briefcase is on the back top bunk. Take my cell phone out of my briefcase and call 911."

"And what do we want, a boat?" she asked.

Nicole moaned. "No boat."

"A chopper, then." Chance said. "That'll be quicker, anyway."

Andi shook her head. "I doubt they could land on our minisize beach."

"Then they'll have to land on our maxisize roof." Chance's smile was grim. "The size of this monster has to come in handy for something."

Andi found Chance's briefcase and decided to stay in the back to make the call so she wouldn't alarm Nicole by whatever she discussed with the operator. Several frustrating minutes later she replaced the phone and hurried down the hallway.

"Are they on their way?" Bowie called out as she walked into the kitchen.

"Not quite." She stopped in her tracks. "What the hell's this?" She stared at Chance stretched out unconscious on the bed and Nicole sitting in a deck chair beside the bed.

"He passed out," Bowie said as he rubbed Nicole's back. "And Nic says she feels better sitting up than lying down."

"Passed out? Is he okay?"

"Sure. He did the same thing in the tenth grade before his big date with Myra Oglethorpe. Intense stress affects him like that sometimes, I guess. He'll come around in a few minutes."

"So he does have a weakness," Andi murmured.

"Yeah, and he's going to hate that this happened to him right now."

Andi turned to Nicole. "You really feel better sitting?"

Nicole nodded. "I think Chance hated seeing me in pain. He—*ah!*" She gripped the arms of the deck chair as another contraction grabbed her.

"By the way," Bowie said, continuing to massage Nicole's back. "What did you mean *not quite* with the chopper? I don't like the sound of *not quite*."

"Our timing's not great. There were several car pileups during a sandstorm on the freeway, and medical helicopters are in short supply. I gave them our approximate location, told them to look for the houseboat wedged sideways on the beach. They said that should make it easy to find us. They'll show up when they can."

"And in the meantime?"

"They asked if we had anyone here with experience delivering babies, and I said yes."

"Unconscious, but experienced," Bowie said.

"I didn't know that he'd passed out. We can hope he comes around, but in the meantime, you'd better go scrub up."

Bowie's gaze locked with hers and she watched the uncertainty fade and the determination grow. She decided she would wake Chance up, if only to witness his brother taking charge of a situation.

While Bowie tried his best to sterilize his hands and arms at the kitchen sink, Andi moved Chance's laptop to the floor, unscrewed the tabletop and converted the second set of benches into a double bed. She kept up a conversation with Nicole as she worked and checked her every few seconds. The pains were very close together.

"I'll get every pillow on the boat, so we can prop you up," she told Nicole. "But I'd feel better if you'd move this program to the bed. Otherwise Fifi's liable to land on the floor, and it's not very clean."

"Fifi?" Nicole managed a weak smile between pains.

"Or Gigi. I figured you'd want to go with something French to please your mother-in-law."

"Oh, Andi." Nicole's eyes rounded in horror. "She's gonna *kill* me for this. She wanted to videotape the birth."

"With subtitles, of course."

Nicole started to giggle. "Andi, thank God you're—oh, sh—" She clapped her hand over her mouth before the swearword came out.

"I'd advise you to go ahead and swear," Andi said. "Trust me, the baby won't pick it up, despite Mrs. Chauncey M.'s theories."

"What theories?" Bowie came around the counter holding his hands in the air.

"Tell you later. You're on duty. I'm going to get pillows. I'll be right back."

"Get my camera!" Nicole called after her as Andi raced down the hall.

10

WHEN ANDI RETURNED with pillows and towels in her arms and the camera shoved down the front of her suit, she found Bowie kneeling in front of Nicole. He was talking to her softly, his hands still in the air to keep them clean, while Nicole dug her fingers into his shoulders.

"Just hang on until it's over," he murmured. "That's it. Quick little breaths."

"I must be hurting you," she gasped out.

"Not at all. Just hold on."

"There." Nicole hung her head and relaxed her grip. "That one's past."

"I'll fix the bed," Andi said, "and then I'll try to wake Sleeping Beauty."

"Yeah, I'd feel better if he was in on this," Bowie said.

Andi walked around them and made a backrest of the pillows as she listened to Bowie help Nicole through another pain. "If you didn't finish the childbirth classes, how do you know the breathing techniques?"

"Watching 'ER,'" he said.

"Thank God for television." Andi set the camera on a nearby shelf, where it would be handy, before crouching in front of Nicole. "I'm going to help you over to the bed now, okay?"

"Okay." Nicole gripped her hand tight when another pain hit.

Wondering if Nicole had the strength to break the bones in her hand, Andi held on until the contraction passed, and then she finally got Nicole settled on the bed. "We'll have to get that bathing suit off, Nic."

"But what if Chance wakes up?"

"Hey, sweetheart, this is no time to be—"

"Let's get her a sheet if it'll make her feel better," Bowie said. "That's how they do it in the hospital, anyway."

"Bowie, I love you," Nicole said, her eyes teary. "Don't you just love him, Andi?"

"Yeah, I'm crazy about him. You got yourself a winner, there, sis." Andi leaned down and kissed Nicole on the cheek. "Sit tight. I'll get you a sheet."

She returned quickly, helped Nicole out of her bathing suit and draped the sheet over her, forming a tent over her bent knees. None too soon, apparently. Just as Andi was adjusting the sheet, Nicole let loose with a swearword Andi had never heard her use before.

Bowie looked startled. "Nic? You okay, babe?"

"Don't you *babe* me," Nicole said, panting. "And wake up that worthless brother of yours. It's showtime."

Andi stifled a chuckle as she looked at Bowie. "Guess I'd better rouse Marcus Welby. Watch over her."

Nicole took one look at her husband, gave a loud groan and started swearing again. "I hate men!" she cried, breathing hard. "Every one of you can take a leap off the Sears Tower, as far as I'm concerned. And take your pride and joy with you!"

Bowie patted her knee. "We will, I promise. Right after we bring another delightful little girl into the world."

"I'm never letting her have sex," Nicole said darkly.

"She'll be a nun," Andi promised as she dampened a kitchen towel at the sink and walked back to the unconscious Chance. She wiped his forehead until he stirred and moaned.

Nicole continued to swear a blue streak during each contraction.

Andi figured her sister must be getting close to zero hour. "Let me know if you need me over there," she said over her shoulder as she applied the damp towel to Chance's face.

"I may need an interpreter," Bowie said.

Andi grinned. "She learned to swear in Italian when Dad was stationed in Sicily. She just told you and Chance where to shove your precious houseboat."

Chance slowly opened his eyes and looked up at her with a dazed expression. "Is that Nicole yelling?"

"Yeah. The paramedics couldn't make it so we're delivering this baby ourselves. We could use your help."

Chance squeezed his eyes shut. "I passed out. Dammit."

"Think you're up to helping us out?"

"Yep." With a grim set to his mouth, he heaved himself to his feet.

"Steady," Andi said as he staggered slightly. She grabbed the chair Nicole had vacated and shoved it under him.

He sat down heavily. "Hi, Nic. How're you doing?"

"Oh, so now I get to deal with two of you Jefferson sleazeballs."

Bowie peered around her tented knees. "But hon, I'm your hero, remember?"

"I'm never letting you hero me again, you slimebucket. Oh, God!"

Chance swallowed and turned pale.

Bowie was concentrating on the task at hand and

seemed not to notice his brother's condition. "What should I do, Chance?" he asked.

"Tell her to push," Chance said, his voice strained. Sweat popped out on his forehead.

"Push," Bowie said, excitement lacing his voice.

Nicole swore some more.

"Push, sweetheart! That's it. She's coming!"

Andi noticed Chance didn't look too good, but she didn't have time to tend to him. She grabbed the camera and stationed herself at the end of the bed. Kneeling down, she looked through the viewfinder as Nicole gave one more colorful curse and Bowie gently eased his daughter into the world. She forgot to click the shutter, and tears blurred her view. The tiny baby began to cry, and so did Bowie.

Andi lowered the camera. Some things just couldn't be captured on film. Bowie lifted the baby, umbilical cord still attached, and laid her against Nicole's breast. Then he leaned down and kissed his wife on the forehead, just as the whir of helicopter blades sounded in the distance and Chance moaned and slipped off the chair onto the floor.

WHEN CHANCE CAME TO he was looking into the face of a paramedic. Dammit, he'd passed out again. Major disgrace. He struggled to sit up.

"Take it easy," the guy said. "Don't move too fast. Fathers pass out all the time during deliveries."

"I'm not the father. I'm the uncle."

"So you're the sensitive type. No reason to be embarrassed about that."

Chance clenched his jaw. "I'm not the sensitive type." He got to his feet and shook his head to clear it. The houseboat was a rush of sound and motion as the medical team worked in its practical and efficient manner to clean up mother and baby and prepare them for the flight to a Las Vegas hospital. Everyone exclaimed over the healthy baby. Nicole wasn't in pain anymore and smiled at everyone who came within her field of vision. Chance felt his strength returning.

It really was a miracle, he thought, catching the contagious spirit of goodwill that touched everyone on board. Bowie ran around slapping the medical-team members on the back and promising to mail them all cigars. His little brother had delivered a baby, Chance thought, while he had been worse than no help. He'd been in the way. All in all, it had been an extremely humbling day.

He watched Andi rush around gathering belongings for Bowie and Nicole to take with them. Then she handed Bowie the key to her apartment so he'd have a place to stay in Las Vegas while Nicole and the baby were in the hospital. Everyone had a duty, a responsibility, except him. He couldn't remember ever feeling quite so useless. Or quite so relieved.

"That does it, then," the woman in charge said, surveying Nicole bundled on a stretcher and the baby tucked into a plastic bassinet. "We'll transport mother, baby and father to the hospital. Here's the phone number." She handed a card to Andi. "I can radio someone to fly in and take you two off tonight, or the marina can send a boat here tomorrow morning. Your choice."

Andi flicked a quick look at Chance. "Are you okay until tomorrow?"

"I'm fine." And he was. With every passing minute he felt stronger...and more foolish. The least he could do to redeem himself was figure out a way to get this boat off the sand. "We can call in the morning if we need help," he added.

"But you're stuck here."

"I may be able to do something about that tomorrow," he said. "I'd like to try."

"Just the two of you, with this huge boat?"

Andi glanced at him. "We'll use leverage," she said.

The woman looked at them with a resigned expression, as if she knew better than to argue with tourists. "Okey-dokey. I guess that's why God made cell phones. Let's go, gang."

"Bowie," Chance said.

His brother turned.

"Hell of a job, Bowie," he said. And for the first time in years, Chance embraced his brother. "Take care of those two."

"With my life," Bowie said, his voice hoarse as he stepped back. Then he hugged Andi as the medics picked up Nicole's stretcher.

"Just a minute," Chance said. "Let me say goodbye to my niece." He hurried over and leaned down toward the tiny child tucked in the bassinet. Andi came up beside him, and he slipped his hand around her waist and drew her in close.

"See you soon, whatever your name is," Chance said, touching his finger to the baby's soft cheek.

"*Au revoir,* Colette," Andi said, flashing a grin at her sister.

"*Colette?*" Bowie said, elbowing nearer. "Where did that come from, Nic? You know I was holding out for Bowina."

"*Bowina?*" Chance stared at his brother.

"I made it up, but it's supposed to be the feminine version of—"

"It's the feminine version of blockhead! You can't name this gorgeous little girl *Bowina*. Not while I'm—"

"Okay, folks," the paramedic said. "You can name her Fred, for all I care, but you'll have to do it on your own time. We're outa here."

Despite his faith in the paramedics, Chance followed them out to the rear deck and watched, the wind from the rotors whipping his hair, as they lifted Nicole and the baby up to the roof and got them safely inside the helicopter.

"I'll call Mom from Las Vegas!" Bowie yelled over his shoulder as he climbed the ladder to the roof of the houseboat.

"And my parents!" Andi cried out as she came to stand beside Chance.

"I'll call everybody!" Bowie called over his shoulder.

As he got into the helicopter, he turned to wave. "Bowina rules!" he shouted, laughing.

"Dream on, idiot!" Chance yelled back.

"You don't have to worry," Andi said from beside him. "Nicole would never let him get away with naming her that."

"To hell with what Nicole would let him do. *I'm* not letting him name her that."

Andi chuckled as the helicopter lifted off over the water, creating a small tidal wave on the surface. "You may not get a vote."

"I may not, at that. Some help I was." He watched the blinking lights of the helicopter as it carried the little family up into the night sky. "Thank God you and Bowie came through."

"I think it all worked out absolutely perfectly."

He continued to gaze after the departing helicopter. "Perfectly? With me passed out most of the time?"

"You bet. With you out of the picture, Bowie got to shine. It may have been his finest moment. If you'd been in charge, as usual, he wouldn't know that he had the strength to handle a crisis like this. Now he does.''

Chance mulled that one over. The implication was pretty clear—he had been one of the obstacles to Bowie taking on his fair share of responsibility. How could he have, when Chance had always grabbed it away from him?

He couldn't see the lights of the helicopter anymore. ''Bowie will be a good father,'' he said. A picture of Bowie cradling the little girl in his arms hit him like a sucker punch in the gut. He wanted what Bowie had. Wanted it bad.

Andi was silent for several seconds as the helicopter lights grew smaller. ''Do you wish you were on that helicopter going with them?'' She sounded subdued.

Her comment took a minute to register. Their situation took a moment longer. Bowie, Nicole and the baby were on their way to Las Vegas, and he and Andi were...

Alone. A quiver of anticipation ran through him as he turned to her. She could ease this empty feeling. She might be the only person in the world who could. Her hair was tangled from the wind created by the helicopter blades, but now only a faint breeze stirred around them. ''No, I wouldn't want to be on that helicopter.''

''You wouldn't?'' She lifted her eyebrows.

Memories of the afternoon came rushing back to heat his blood and tighten his groin. Those thoughts, combined with the need to hold and be held, created a desire so strong it took his breath away. An answering need flashed in her eyes and suddenly they were locked in each other's arms, their mouths seeking, their hands searching, unfastening, stroking.

''I could take you right here,'' he said, gasping. ''Right on this damn deck.''

She pushed her hand inside his shorts. "We have ten beds—oh, yes, touch me there—ten beds, inside."

No. He didn't want to make love inside that crazy place where so much had just happened, where he'd been so weak he'd passed out in the middle of the action. With superhuman effort, he wrenched away. "The roof. Go on up. I'll get what I need."

She stared at him as she struggled for breath. "The roof? Why on earth do you want to go up on the roof?"

He gazed at her as an image of making love under a canopy of stars fueled his imagination. "I have my reasons."

"Name one."

God, she was saucy. And he loved it. Needed that spirit to lift him up. "I want to see your naked body caressed by starlight as you lie beneath me."

"Oh." Excitement flared in her eyes. "Well, okay, but we could—"

"I want to hear your moans echo between the rock walls of this inlet."

She sighed. He'd pulled her bathing suit half-off and her breasts quivered as she took a deep breath and gazed up at him. "Oh."

"And I want you to be able to look up and see the whole universe while I'm deep inside you."

Her lips parted, but no exclamation came out this time.

He smiled. Finally, he'd made her speechless. It was worth slowing down the action, just for that. "Cat got your tongue, Andi? Better find it. I also want to feel the lick of your tongue, and the press of your lips, on every inch of—"

"Go," she said in a breathless whisper. "I'll be waiting."

"On the roof?"

"I can't think of a place I'd rather be."

Neither could he, he thought moments later as he climbed the ladder carrying their sleeping bags. The contents of his general-store purchase rested in the pocket of his shorts.

But the roof was empty.

He tossed down the sleeping bags and looked around. "Andi?"

"I want to stroke my hands over your starlit, naked body," she said.

"Where are you?"

"And then I want to flick my tongue over every delicious inch of you," she said, her voice drifting up from somewhere below him.

"Then you'll have to get the hell up on the roof, which is where I am, woman."

"And I want your moan to echo between the rock walls when I finally put my mouth over your—"

"Andi!" His cry echoed back to him. He was going wild.

Slowly she appeared, coming up the ladder. She'd changed out of her swimsuit and put on the sexiest underwear he'd ever seen—wispy bits of black lace that barely covered her nipples and the vee between her thighs. And she was carrying an open jar of something. "Gotcha," she whispered.

"You had to do some sneaking to get behind me like that." But he had trouble being angry when he was so damn aroused.

"Oh, I'm very good at sneaking." She reached between her breasts and unfastened a catch that allowed the skimpy bra to fall away. She shrugged out of it and it fell in her wake. "And I should also tell you, before we get too involved and you might forget, that I'm terrible at taking orders, and I hate letting someone else get the upper hand.''

He gazed at her, off balance as he usually was when this woman was around. ''What's in the jar?''

''Fingerpaints.''

He peered closer. ''Looks like fudge sauce to me.''

''Does it?'' She dipped her fingers into the jar as she came toward him. ''Does that mean we don't get to paint? You said you liked doing that.'' Her breasts swayed provocatively as she approached.

He ached for her. ''We may not have time.''

''I'll let you paint, too.'' She stopped in front of him and smeared sauce around his nipple. Then she tilted her head to one side. ''Nice design, but I can improve on it.'' She started making swirling patterns, kneading his skin with her fingers.

He couldn't believe what the sensation did to him, how his loins began to pound as she played with her design. And then she began to lick him clean, murmuring her appreciation as if she were enjoying a piece of Godiva.

His breathing grew labored. ''Andi...''

She lifted her head and held up the jar. ''Sorry,'' she said, her tone low and sultry as she slowly sucked the chocolate from her fingers. ''Didn't mean to hog all the fun. Your turn.''

He took the jar. He couldn't remember ever touching fudge sauce with his fingers, and it felt creamy and sinful as he scooped some out.

She shook her hair back over her shoulders and cupped her breasts with both hands. ''Your canvas.''

He set the jar at his feet. Then he straightened and began painting the sauce on as if she were wearing a fudge bikini top. Her nipples tightened as he swirled and smoothed the sauce, and the visual and tactile pleasure of smearing the fudge over her breasts drove him crazy. She'd lured him into creating the sweetest treat he could ever imagine taking into his mouth. Finally he could wait no longer. Easing her supporting hands away, he cradled one chocolate-covered breast in his hand and began to taste his handiwork.

"Good?" she murmured, arching upward.

"Mmm." He licked and suckled and went slowly out of his mind. "Mmm-mmm."

He wasn't exactly clear how they got there, but somehow they'd ended up on their knees as he continued to feast on her breasts. He was so engrossed he barely noticed when she unfastened his shorts and pulled down his briefs. Then she demanded another turn, and he found himself stretched out flat, the stars above him, the roof of the houseboat under him. He had the first fudge-covered erection of his life.

And indeed, his moans did echo against the canyon walls as she enjoyed her chocolate-coated treat, comparing him favorably to every candy bar she'd ever known. Through the unbelievable bliss of her nibbling forays, he fought to keep some kind of control.

"Snack time's over," he said finally, gasping as he drew her away and brought her up to plunder her mouth with his lips and tongue. "You are outrageous."

"Is that good?" she murmured, nibbling on his lower lip.

"Good doesn't even begin to cover it." He rolled her gently to her back. "But I don't want to fingerpaint anymore."

"Time for a new game?"

"The oldest game of all." He slipped his hand beneath the black lace of her panties as he licked some lingering smears of fudge from her breasts. "Even better than chocolate."

"You'll have to prove it to me."

"Love to." He drew in a breath as he slid two fingers deep into her moistness and felt the tremor go through her. He nuzzled her ear as he created a subtle friction with his fingers and another tremor shook her. "I don't think it'll take long to prove," he whispered.

"Ha. I'm cool…as a cucumber." Her breathing grew uneven. "If you can last forever, so can I."

"I have a reason to last forever." There it was again. She pulsed against his fingers. Soon. "You don't."

"Pride," she whispered. "Oh, Chance, that's…I don't want you to think…ohhh…to think I'm a…pushover."

"Never." He settled his lips over her mouth and drank in her cries as he propelled her over the edge. Then, as she gradually returned to earth, he eased her panties off and reached behind him to find the shorts she'd stripped away during the fingerpainting session.

"My pride is gone," she murmured as he sheathed himself. "I still want you."

"I was hoping you would." Cradling her head on his arm, he moved over her and eased between her sleek thighs. His heart hammered frantically in anticipation of burying himself within her heat at last. He gazed into her eyes, those wise, funny, passionate eyes. "I'm very glad you still want me."

"I do." She grasped his hips and drew him down. "Show me the universe, Chance."

He pushed deep, and he thought his heart might stop altogether from the sweet ecstasy of the moment. He looked down at her, and she seemed as awestruck as he, but the shadows hid her expression from him. "I wish I could see your face better," he murmured.

She swallowed and took a shaky breath. "You can't because it's dark."

"Thank you, Einstein," he said softly, leaning down to kiss her. "Oh, well. Tomorrow we'll have sunlight." He eased back and buried himself again, and as he did, she lifted her hips and welcomed him with an undulating motion that made him gasp with delight. It was the most sensuous joining he'd ever known.

"Tomorrow we...have to move...the boat," she said between ragged breaths.

"Who gives a damn about the boat?" He abandoned himself to the exquisite pleasure of matching her rhythm and discovering which movements brought forth her lusty moans.

Vaguely he realized he'd just turned away from responsibility once again, and that doing so was becoming a dangerous habit. Then she tightened around him and began crooning his name, and he no longer cared. The drive for satisfaction crowded out all rational thought, until at last the sounds of their joyous completion careened off the surrounding canyon walls and floated up into the star-sprinkled night.

11

WRAPPED IN Chance's arms, satiated by his lovemaking, Andi drifted into a light sleep beneath the glow of a million stars. A gentle rocking motion only increased her sense of well-being as the stars gradually faded and the sky lightened to the color of antique pearls.

"Oh, dammit!"

Andi came fully awake with a start. "Chance?"

He was on all fours staring around him. "Un-frigging-believable."

"What?"

He crawled over to where the unused sleeping bags lay in a heap, grabbed one and threw it at her. "Wrap up. We're in the middle of the lake."

"No!" She pulled the sleeping bag around her and sat up. Sure enough, water stretched on all sides of the boat. The shore seemed very far away, and the pattern of rocks and mountains was unfamiliar. "What happened?"

He struggled into his discarded shorts. "Maybe the helicopter setting down dislodged us."

"Or maybe you did." She smiled. "You were pretty enthusiastic there at the end, Romeo."

He zipped his shorts and glanced at her. "You weren't exactly passive yourself, Juliet."

"I *knew* we could get the boat unstuck. See how things have a way of working out?"

"Yeah, this is just peachy." Chance squinted in all directions. "We just have to hope the remaining propeller works, and that we have enough gas to cruise around and figure out which little dimple in that shoreline is the cove where we left half our stuff. We're in terrific shape."

"You worry too much." Andi refused to let a little glitch spoil her contentment. The lake was calm, the footing on the houseboat roof good. Deciding to celebrate her newfound joy in the fresh light of dawn, she tossed aside the sleeping bag, stood and spread her arms. "Hey, world, *qué pasa?*"

Chance gazed at her. "We also have to hope that the guys in the fishing boat coming up behind us don't have binoculars."

Andi dropped like a stone, scrambled for the sleeping bag and crawled completely under it. She lifted up a corner and glared out at him. "You might have warned me, Chance Jefferson."

He grinned. "I would have, if I'd had any idea you were planning your own special salute to the sun."

She poked her head out. "Are they coming closer?"

"Yeah, they are, as a matter of fact."

She pulled the sleeping bag over her head with a groan. "Wave them off," she said through the layers of the bag.

He lifted a section to peer at her. "What?"

"Wave them off! And stop talking to me! I don't want them to know I'm under here."

"Hell, I'm waving them in. I want to ask which way the marina is from here so I can orient myself."

"Chance Jefferson, don't you dare call those fishermen over here while I'm lying naked under this sleeping bag."

He pulled the edge of the bag up again. "What did you say? I can't hear you through all that down filling."

"Scat! Vamoose!" She grabbed the edge of the sleeping bag from his hand and jerked it over her head. The soft growl of the fishing boat's motor drew nearer.

He patted her bottom. "Relax. You worry too much."

"Oooh! Wait'll I get my hands on you!"

"That sounds promising." He squeezed her through the sleeping bag.

"Don't touch me!" Grasping the sleeping bag in both hands, she crawled on her belly away from him like a paratrooper.

"Subtle, Andi," he said. "Nobody will ever guess you're under there dragging that thing all over the roof. They'll just think I bought myself a motorized sleeping bag."

The sound of the approaching boat changed from a steady drone to the putt, putt of an idling engine. "Yo, buddy!" called an unfamiliar male voice. "You got problems?"

Andi scrunched her eyes closed and prayed the conversation would be brief.

It wasn't. She lay under the increasingly hot sleeping bag for what seemed like hours as the men laughed and joked. A sneeze tortured her for several minutes before she beat down the urge. She couldn't hear what the men were saying, and the hotter and more cramped she became, the more certain she was that they were laughing and joking about her. As time dragged on, she planned elaborate tortures for Chauncey M. Jefferson the Fourth.

After an eternity the idling motor roared to life and the fishermen left.

The edge of the sleeping bag lifted. "They're gone," Chance whispered.

She threw back the suffocating material and sat up, her patience frayed. "You were making fun of me hiding under here, weren't you?"

"No, we—"

"I'll just bet. I'll bet you all had a good laugh about the bimbo under the blanket."

He crouched and smiled as he tried to gather her close. "You look so cute and ruffled. Honest, I wouldn't—"

She shoved him away. "Then why did you take so long?"

"Because." He reached for her again. "Come here."

"Because you didn't care if I was under there, did you? Because you get a kick out of all these scrapes I get myself into."

"I do, but—" He lost his balance and reached for her all in one movement, so that she toppled onto him as he rolled to his back. His arms tightened around her. "Stop struggling or we'll both flip over this little six-inch railing into the water. Knowing you, it's a miracle it hasn't happened already."

She stopped struggling. Falling into the lake from the top of the houseboat would not be a good way to start the day. "See, you think I'm a brainless klutz."

"Not brainless."

"But a klutz." She supported her chin on her hand so she could look at him. His eyes were warm and full of humor, and despite her irritation, the brush of his chest hair against her bare breasts felt very good.

He smiled. "An adorable klutz. And don't forget you're talking to the guy who passed out when he was supposed to help deliver a baby."

"Twice."

"I see I won't have to worry about you forgetting. You'll probably blackmail me with it."

"Thanks for the idea." She laid her cheek over his heart and listened to its steady beat. "So you weren't joking about me with those guys?"

"Of course not." He rolled them both over gently, so they weren't so close to the rail and he was propped above her. "There. That makes me a little less nervous. It's a damn good thing neither of us stumbled around in the middle of the night looking for the bathroom."

"If you weren't talking about me, what took you so long while those fishermen were here? I was beginning to think you'd discovered a couple of fraternity brothers."

"Just playing the good ol' boy game." He stroked her hair back from her face. "I had to let them carry on about me floating in the middle of the lake all alone on a ten-person houseboat."

"They really thought you were alone?"

"Yep." He kissed her on the nose. "I pretended my buddies were back on the beach, clueless that the boat had drifted during the night with me on the roof. I implied there was a lot of beer involved. Yeah, they thought I was alone. I didn't see any sign of binoculars in their boat, either." He gazed down at her. "Looks like the dawn flasher was only seen by me."

"Thank you for checking on the binocular situation. That makes me feel better."

"Me, too. I'm a little proprietary about my Lady Godiva." He stroked her breast. "You're still sticky."

"We need a swim or something."

"Or something." He leaned down to give her a few swipes of his tongue as he continued to talk, and the stubble of his beard prickled tantalizingly against her skin. "I also described the cove to them, and they gave me directions how to get back. I figured if I brushed them off too fast, they'd start wondering if I had a dead body under the sleeping bag. If anyone took the time to notice, you were a strange-looking bundle under there."

"A strange-looking bundle. How flattering."

He eased his hips between her thighs. "Ah, but you're also the prettiest bundle I've ever found naked under a sleeping bag." Beneath the cotton of his shorts, his arousal was evident.

"Chance, I really think we should—"

"Funny how the same thing keeps happening whenever I'm near you like this."

"Hysterical. Shouldn't we be testing the motors or something?"

"I'm testing yours." He raised up enough to unzip his shorts, although he left the waistband buttoned.

"Chance! Another boat could come along, and it's almost broad daylight."

"I'll listen for boats." He pulled a condom from his pocket.

"Oh, sure you will. Let's go below." She found herself growing moist and ready, despite her misgivings about his latest plan.

"If we're inside the boat I really wouldn't see anyone coming. This way I'll know if we're alone out here or not." He handed her the condom. "Open this for me."

"You're really serious!"

"Did you doubt it?"

"Of course I doubted it!"

"Where's that wild spirit of yours, Andi?"

"You really plan to make love on top of a houseboat in the middle of a lake in broad daylight?" But the idea excited her tremendously.

"Yeah, if I can get some cooperation. Open the condom and help me put it on."

She did. The open zipper of his shorts brushed against her thigh as he slipped deep inside her.

"You're beyond crazy," she murmured.

He eased back and thrust forward again. "That's how you make me, fudge woman, beyond crazy."

Her body welcomed him, rising to meet his thrust even as her mind said she should make him stop. "I can't believe we're doing this."

As he gazed into her eyes, he settled into the insistent rhythm that had carried her away so completely the night before. "And I can't believe you're still talking."

"I just think...mmm." She quivered as he made firm contact with her most sensitive spot.

"Yes?"

"Never mind," she whispered as he continued his deep, deliberate strokes. "Just keep doing that."

"I thought I might."

As the tension mounted within her, she held his gaze. The tenderness in his eyes revealed that this joining was about more than pleasure, although the pleasure was incredible. A rush of joy surged through her, heightening her response.

"Oh, Andi," he murmured, lowering his mouth to hers.

Her name had never sounded so sweet. No kiss had ever touched her soul like this one. He slowed the pace, as if to draw out the last moments, and then, in response to one mighty thrust, she surrendered to a shattering climax. He caught her cries against his mouth and mingled them with his own as his release shuddered through him.

FALLING IN LOVE with Andi wasn't a great idea, but Chance didn't seem to be able to stop himself. At the beginning of this trip, he'd thought he could avoid becoming involved with her sexually. Then, once that stronghold had fallen before the onslaught of her incredible appeal, he'd thought he could avoid becoming involved with her emotionally.

Yet, as he piloted the boat in the direction of the little cove and Andi busied herself clearing away the confusion from the night before, he kept catching her hand as she went past him and pulling her over for a kiss. The kisses weren't so much for sexual stimulation, although they definitely gave him that, but for the joy of connecting with her and feeling that surge of electricity between them.

They had decided on an agenda—moor at the cove, call the hospital to check on Nicole and the baby, then load everything they'd left on the sand, assuming it was all still there. Beyond that, they'd made no plan. Logically they should take the boat into the marina and drive into Vegas to see Nicole. Logically they should end the vacation today. He'd agreed to the trip in order to fulfill Bowie's birthday wish. Bowie wasn't even here anymore.

But Chance didn't want to turn the boat in. It seemed to be running fine even with one propeller pretty well chewed up. He'd hauled in the trailing mooring lines and miraculously the stakes had still been tied to them. The wind had died down, there was food in the refrigerator, and ten beds. He felt the urge to try them all.

He spied the little cove up ahead. "Land, ho!" he called out to Andi, who was putting away pillows in the back.

"Is anybody there on our beach?"

"Nope." *Our beach.* He'd like to make it that. The cove was secluded and there certainly wasn't room for another houseboat to moor, which meant they'd have a lot of privacy. But Andi probably wanted to go visit Nicole and the baby. Although he'd seen a soft light in her eyes this morning when they'd made love on the roof, he wasn't sure how to interpret it.

She came up beside him. "There's our stuff! The deck

chairs, and the fire circle, and the cooler and beach towels. Everything's there, thank goodness.''

"I figured it would be. We haven't been gone that long.''

"I know, but it seems like years since we sat down on that beach and read excerpts from Nicole's book.''

"Yeah, it does.'' He'd been falling in love with her then, but he hadn't wanted to admit it to himself. Sharing the birth of the baby, knowing she accepted the vulnerability he'd shown through the crisis, and then making incredible love, twice, pretty much clinched it for him. And everything would be terrific—as long as they stayed on this houseboat for the rest of their lives. That's where the problem lay. He couldn't picture her in Chicago putting up with his stress-filled schedule and he sure as hell wasn't moving to Nevada.

"Hang on,'' he said. "I'm going to ram it up on the beach.''

"And I bet you love doing that, too. What a thrill, sitting at the controls of this long, massive boat, and then shoving it deep into that soft, yielding sand. What a macho power trip.''

She sure had a way with words. He lost all interest in beaching the boat in favor of the act it symbolized. But the job had to be done. He grinned at her. "Just to prove that I don't need this macho power trip, I'm going to let you ram it up on the beach.''

"Yeah? Cool.''

"Get over here, and bring your testosterone.''

She popped into the seat the minute he vacated it. "How fast?''

"I'll let you decide. But don't be tentative. You don't want us sliding back out.''

"God, no.'' She chuckled. "Nothing worse than that.''

He watched her settle into the task, her expression intent.

"Give me a little direction, at least," she said.

"Okay. The technique I've used is to go in slow and make sure your aim is good, and then, just before you hit the beach, gun it. You should end up nice and tight."

"Oh, I bet. I love it when you talk dirty."

"You started this. I was only beaching the boat."

"Sure."

He had a feeling that the longer he hung around Andi, the more he'd adopt her sexy, playful view of the world, and the tougher it would be to concentrate on the serious business of running a huge company. He couldn't pay attention during a stockholders' meeting if he found himself daydreaming in sexual metaphors.

"Here we go," she said, her voice humming with excitement.

He gripped the console as the motors roared, the boat hit the beach and the prow dug firmly into the sand.

She let out a whoop of triumph.

"That's great! Shut 'er down. Let's moor this puppy."

"Are you gonna drive those long stakes into the ground?" Her smile twinkled at him.

He threw his arm around her shoulders and treated himself to a fast, hard kiss. "What do you have, a one-track mind?"

"Don't you?"

He gazed at her. She'd put on a T-shirt and shorts for the trip into the cove. There was nothing particularly sexy about the outfit, but all he had to do was concentrate on her for two minutes and he was hard and aching. "At the moment, yes," he said.

12

ANDI HELD THE STAKES while Chance swung the sledge-hammer. One glancing blow and he could have broken one of her fingers, but she never feared that he might miss and hit her hand.

She helped him wind the mooring ropes around the stakes, and then she dusted off her hands. "Should we start loading, or call the hospital first?"

Chance took off his sunglasses and wiped his arm over his sweaty forehead. Then he replaced his glasses. "Before we do either one, let's talk about a few things."

Andi panicked. They were coming to the end of the trip. They'd load up the stuff, call the hospital and take the boat back to the marina. Despite the look he'd had in his eyes when they'd made love this morning, when push came to shove, he wasn't interested in a yoga teacher from Las Vegas. He probably wanted to make sure she understood that although he'd had a great time, everything would end when he left Nevada, because he had a business to run. She'd told herself to expect this, yet she'd forgotten in the excitement of loving Chance.

She remembered what he'd said a moment ago, when she'd asked him if he had a one-track mind. *At the moment, yes.* The moment had come to an end.

She decided to preempt him and salvage her pride. She walked over to the semicircle of chairs and sat down in a deliberately nonchalant pose. "You know, this has been great fun, but when you get right down to it, totally out of the realm of reality.''

''That's true.'' He looked at her with some wariness.

She leaned back in the chair and forced a small laugh. ''We're two adults, and should be able to have a little flirtation without turning it into a federal case.''

''I guess so.''

''Well, just so you know, there's no pressure from my side of this equation. It's been great, but hardly enough to build a future on. We're too different. I mean, you have a company to run and I have...my own crazy life to live, right?''

''Mmm.'' He turned to look out over the water. ''I can't argue with your logic.''

''I didn't expect you to.'' She swallowed the lump in her throat. What had she imagined, that he'd drop to his knees and pledge his undying love? That he'd abandon his megamillion-dollar company and sell shoes in Las Vegas, just to be with her?

''The only thing is—''

''What?'' she asked too quickly.

He turned to look at her. ''The boat's rented for a week.''

She told herself not to grasp at straws. ''Are you worried about whether we'll get a refund if we return it early?''

''No, I'm not, dammit. After all we've been through, do you still think I'm that focused on the bottom line?''

''Well, I—''

''Don't answer that. I'm trying to find out if you have any interest in...keeping the houseboat a little longer.''

She grasped at a whole handful of straws. ''With you on it?''

He grinned. ''No, all by yourself.'' He walked over to

her chair and leaned his hands on the arms, which brought him very close. "You and a ten-person houseboat. Of course with me on it, you nut!"

A reprieve. A person with any self-respect would reject a few more days, knowing the ending would be exactly the same. But as he leaned over her, his very kissable mouth inches from hers, all she wanted to do was gobble him up. "I would be very interested in that."

"Good. So would I."

She couldn't keep the big smile off her face. By the end of the week she might be in tears, but in the meantime, she would party hearty.

"There's the matter of Nicole and the baby," he said, pushing himself upright again. "If she needs us there for any reason, or if you want to drive into Vegas and see them, we could dock at the marina for a day or so."

"I guess we could. If she needs us." If she didn't, Andi knew she'd rather stay here with Chance. That's how far gone she was. "If she doesn't need us, I was planning to spend a week in Chicago with her after the baby was born, anyway, so it's not like I won't have the opportunity to play aunt."

"And once I'm back in Chicago, I'll have plenty of opportunities to play uncle."

"But not much time to play houseboat," Andi said.

"No." He smiled gently. "This is it."

"Then I guess we'd better make the most of it, huh? We could drive all over this lake, take in all the sights, and—"

"Or we could stay right here for the next three days." Taking off his sunglasses, he pulled her out of the chair and drew her into his arms. "I like these sights just fine."

She gazed up at him, her heart pounding. "You realize

that means no more ramming the boat into the sand and no more driving the stakes into the ground.''

"Yeah." He cupped her bottom and held her tight as his manhood stirred against her. "I'll have to find other outlets for my testosterone surges."

"Oh."

He gave her a lingering kiss that left her throbbing. "But first we need to call the hospital." He released her and headed for the boat. "I'll get the cell phone." He turned and walked backward, twirling his sunglasses in one hand as he continued talking to her. "The paramedic gave you a card with the number on it. Where is it?"

"It's—Chance, look out!"

Too late. He flipped backward as the taut mooring rope caught him behind the knees and he landed with a crunch on the sand.

She hurried to his side. "Are you okay?"

He got to his feet and glanced down at the mangled sunglasses he'd just sat on. "Yeah, but I doubt if my shades will pull through."

"I'll bet they were expensive."

He took her by the shoulders. "Will you stop implying I give a damn about money? The only time I care about the cost of things is when it negatively affects the business or my family. How come nobody *gets* that?"

"Maybe because you're so busy playing with figures, you don't take the time to tell them."

"They should *know*. But maybe you're right. I'll try to remember to say it, too."

"But in order for them to really believe you, you'll have to stop playing with figures all the time. Actions speak louder, and all that stuff."

"But if I don't handle those things, nobody else will!"

Andi gazed at him silently for a moment and wondered

if he'd already forgotten Bowie's heroics during the baby's birth. "Are you absolutely sure of that?"

Uncertainty flickered in his eyes.

"I didn't think so," she said.

"Well, something weird is happening, at any rate. I'm not in the habit of knocking food into the fire and flipping backward over mooring ropes. Not to mention finding myself in the middle of the lake without a clue."

"It's probably all my fault." She sincerely hoped that was true. Maybe he was turning into a klutz around her for the same reason she became one around him.

"No, I just need to stop acting like an idiot. Where did you say that card was?"

She sighed. No revelation yet. "It's on the kitchen counter, I think."

He stooped to pick up the broken glasses. "I'll be right back. And after we call the hospital, I need to call the office."

"Okay, you do that." So he thought he could settle right back into his old role, did he? Not while she had something to say about it. Until proven otherwise, she'd assume he was becoming disaster-prone because she distracted the hell out of him. And if she had any influence over him, she damn well wasn't going to spend three days watching a man work on his laptop.

Moments later he hopped down from the boat and came toward the chair where she'd gone to await his return. He held the cell phone in one hand and two pop-top cans of orange juice in the other. Barefoot and dressed only in his shorts, he didn't look much like a man dedicated to business pursuits, she thought. With his well-sculpted pecs and rakish stubble, he looked like an international playboy.

He tossed her a can of juice. "Breakfast."

"Thanks. Maybe I should have warned you earlier that Nicole's the domestic goddess, not me. With her gone I can't promise we'll have a well-balanced menu."

"Don't be so modest." He handed her the phone and the card with the number on it before plopping onto a deck chair next to hers. "I happen to know you're a regular Julia Child with fudge sauce." He opened his juice can and took a long swallow.

"I didn't say I wasn't creative." She glanced at him, enjoying the sexy ripple of his throat as he tipped his head back and closed his eyes to drink the juice. "Just not well-balanced."

He finished the juice and crumpled the can. "I'll take creative over well-balanced any day," he said, giving her a very suggestive smile.

She absorbed the implications of that smile and decided that she was definitely capable of keeping him from disappearing into his corporate fog, at least most of the time.

"Make your call," he prompted gently.

"Right." She peered at the card the paramedic had given them and punched in the number. Within a few seconds she was connected with Nicole, who answered the phone with gusto.

"Hey, Nic! Wow, you sound great," Andi said.

"I feel great. The doctor said it was because I didn't take any kind of drugs during delivery. It was a little rough at the time, though, and I guess I swore a tiny bit, huh?"

Andi couldn't resist. "Why do you suppose Chance passed out again?"

"No, really? Did I use the F-word?"

"Are you kidding? That was one of the milder ones. It's all Chance and I have been talking about ever since."

"Oh, God! I'm so embarrassed. Tell Chance I don't usually do that, please!"

"I told him he'd finally seen the real you."

"You didn't! Andi Lombard, so help me, if I weren't in this hospital bed, I'd—"

"Oh, relax," Andi said, laughing. "Seeing you let loose like that was one of the highlights of the evening. And Chance hasn't commented on it once. I don't know if he even noticed, as woozy as he was the whole time."

"You are a rat. I'm telling Mom."

"No, you're not, because then you'll have to adm... all that swearing. Just think what it would have been like if Mom or Mrs. Chauncey M. had been around with a video camera. And sound."

"It would have been completely different because I would have asked for about a million drugs. But I'm sorta glad I couldn't have them, because I don't have any side effects. Chandi's bright and alert, too."

Andi sat up straighter. *"Who?"*

"Chandi. Your niece. My daughter."

"Chandi?" Andi stared at Chance, who was shaking his head frantically and turning both thumbs down.

"Don't you love it? Bowie and I came up with it during the helicopter ride."

"Because they started giving you drugs on the helicopter, right?"

"No! Bowie and I were completely serious."

"That's one opinion. Listen, it's not written down or anything, yet, is it? Like on a birth certificate."

"It most certainly is. Signed, sealed, witnessed. Chandi Bowina Jefferson."

"Oh, God." Andi was torn between horror and hysterics. "Forget all those childbirth courses they offer. There should be mandatory classes in how to name a baby. You and Bowie shouldn't have been turned loose on that birth certificate without supervision.''

Nicole laughed. "Give yourself time to get used to it. After all, you and Chance are going to be the godparents, so a combination of your names is exactly what Bowie and I wanted. And I'm not crazy about the middle name, but Bowie loves it, and she won't have to use it much. Trust me, it's a great name.''

"For a first-round draft pick of the Chicago Bulls, maybe. Did you ask poor Chandi Bowina how she feels?'' Andi heard a crash and looked over to see Chance on the sand, his chair tipped over backward.

"Chandi *Bowina?*'' he said, scrambling to his feet. "Give me that phone.''

"Oh, Uncle Chance has a few words to say.'' She handed him the phone, holding her palm over the speaker. "Don't get too carried away now. Remember, she's a new mommy,'' she murmured.

"Oh, like you didn't tease the devil out of her about the swearing.'' He took the phone. "Nicole? What the hell is this Chandi Bowina nonsense?''

"That was subtle,'' Andi said.

Chance scowled at her, and then, as he listened to Nicole, his mouth dropped open. "You're kidding.'' He rolled his eyes. "Engraved, huh? Yeah, she likes to do that kind of thing.''

He covered the mouthpiece. "My mother loves the name,'' he murmured to Andi. "She's already had a silver cup engraved with it.''

Andi shook her head in disbelief.

He cradled the phone against his shoulder and picked up the deck chair he'd tipped over in his agitation. "Well, if she likes it, and you like it, I guess I like it.'' He covered the mouthpiece again. "Mom thinks the name sounds French."

Andi smothered a laugh.

"Yeah, I suppose we'll all get used to it by the time she's, say, thirty-two." Chance paused and nodded. "Sure. Listen, Nic, do you need us to drive in there and help out with anything?" He glanced at Andi.

She held up her crossed fingers.

"Yeah, we got the boat unstuck." He rocked back on his heels and stared up at the cloudless sky. "Actually, it came loose pretty easy. I think the chopper affected it."

Andi grinned at him.

"Well, if you don't need us for anything, we were considering just finishing out the week with the boat." He listened for a moment. "You're sure? Then I guess we will."

Andi leaped up and started doing her version of an end-zone victory dance.

Chance smiled at her. "But we can certainly drive in if you need us to," he added, giving Andi the thumbs-up sign. "Yeah, Andi said she was planning to fly to Chicago for a visit pretty soon." His smile faded as he continued to listen. Then he sighed. "Yeah, I know that, Nic. Okay, here she is."

Andi took the phone back. "You're sure you don't need us?"

"First tell me how it's going with His Stuffed-Shirtedness," Nicole said.

"Okay."

"I can tell he wants to stay, but do you?"

Andi blew out a breath. "Yeah, I do."

"Look, I certainly don't need you to run in here. In fact, we may try to book a flight out the day after tomorrow. But I worry about you. Bowie says this is the perfect thing, you two being stranded alone together like "Gilligan's Island" or something, but I'm not so sure. I wanted to be around to referee."

"Nicole Lombard Jefferson! I wondered if you'd planned this."

"Not the part where I gave birth on a houseboat. But Bowie and I did think that maybe, if you and Chance got to know each other..."

"Forget it, Nic. Bad plan."

"But you're going to finish out the week with him. That must mean that things are progressing."

"Only to a point. I'm not stupid."

"Well, if that idiot doesn't beg you to marry him, he is extremely stupid. Whoops, they're ready to bring Chandi in for another feeding, so I'd better go. Can you call back tonight? I should know by then when we're leaving."

"Sure, we'll do that."

"Take care of yourself, Andi."

"I will. Bye." She clicked off the phone and handed it to Chance, who was watching her intently. "You said something about checking in at the office, I think."

He set the phone on his chair and came over to rest both hands on her shoulders as he gazed into her eyes. "Is staying with me for the next three days going to be a problem for you?"

She took a deep breath "No. I want to."

"Nicole wanted to make sure I wouldn't hurt you by leading you on with no intention of—"

"That's ridiculous." Andi lifted her chin. "Sometimes Nicole makes the mistake of thinking everyone wants what she wants."

"You mean, a husband and a baby."

"Yeah."

His gaze searched hers. "But you don't want those things?"

The truth hit her like a blow. She wanted a husband and baby more than anything in the world, and in the past few hours she'd even settled on an unlikely candidate to provide both. But she certainly couldn't tell him that. "Maybe someday, but not now, when there's so much fun and adventure to be enjoyed." The lie made her heart ache, but telling it was the only way to keep her pride intact at the end of the week.

"I guess it would take somebody quite unusual to make you give up the freedom you love so much."

"Yes, I guess it would." *And here you are.*

He looked deep into her eyes, and for a moment it seemed as if he might say something more. Instead, he released her and stepped back. "I need to call the office. They're going to wonder what happened to me."

"Tell them you were kidnapped by gypsies," Andi said, and started over toward the boat. "I'm going to make coffee and rustle us up something to eat."

THE GYPSY EXPLANATION wouldn't be far wrong, Chance thought as Andi walked over to the boat and hoisted herself back up on deck. Andi was definitely a free spirit with no desire to be tied down. That was perfect, because she'd never fit into his life anyway. At least, that's what he was busy telling himself as he stared at the cell phone without dialing.

No, it wasn't perfect at all. He sighed and leaned back in the deck chair, closing his eyes so he could think. What he wanted, if he were brutally honest with himself, was to have Andi come to live in Chicago, whether she'd distract him from his work or not. He had a feeling his obsession with her was going to distract him even if he didn't have her physically there. So what was he thinking? Marriage? Ha. She'd just announced that she wasn't interested.

Maybe, if he continued to satisfy her sexually, she'd consider becoming his mistress. That would be better than nothing, but he had a growing conviction it wouldn't be nearly enough. And it wouldn't sit well with Bowie and Nicole, either. No doubt about it, they'd push for a wedding ceremony. The idea intrigued him more than a little. Too bad it intrigued her not at all.

He could smell coffee brewing, and he opened his eyes and sat up straight. He wasn't getting anywhere running around this mental squirrel cage, anyhow, so he might as well make that call to the office. With a sigh he punched in the number and put the phone to his ear. The office phone had just started to ring when Andi reappeared on deck with a broom, and dressed in the red suit she'd worn the first day. She swept the deck vigorously.

"Chance Jefferson's office. Can you hold, please?" Annalise said on the other end.

"Sure." As he listened to canned music, he continued to watch Andi, and damned if she didn't lie down on the deck and start doing her yoga exercises. Through the open railing gate he could see the whole performance as she twisted and turned that luscious body. Oh, God. He disconnected the phone.

13

ANDI HAD HOPED her ploy of yoga exercises on the deck would shorten Chance's business call. She hadn't meant to prevent him from calling altogether. She didn't discover what had happened until after they'd made love on Chance's bed and polished off a breakfast of scrambled eggs, coffee and toast.

"How are they surviving at the office without you?" she asked as they cleared away the dishes.

"I don't know." Chance set the dishes on the counter and got out the dish soap. "I hung up before I talked to anybody."

She almost dropped the carafe of coffee. "You hung up? Why?"

He set the bottle of soap on the counter and turned to her, his glance roving from her head to her toes. His eyes glinted with appreciation. "I think it was the inverted-vee position that did it."

"You didn't even talk to your secretary?"

"Nope." He turned back to the sink and started filling it with warm water and soapsuds.

"Well, now I feel guilty."

He chuckled. "I wondered if you were deliberately trying to sabotage me."

Whoops. "Uh, not exactly. I mean, I do like to start the day with yoga exercises, and the deck has the most space."

"It's okay, Andi." He dumped the breakfast dishes in the soapy water and looked over at her. "Do your damnedest. If I don't have the willpower to ignore you, that's my problem. I have a couple of projects to finish on the laptop before I go back to Chicago, and I plan to spend some time on them today. Trust me, when I'm really concentrating, you could dance naked in front of me and I wouldn't notice."

"I see." Her eyes narrowed. This ol' boy didn't know her all that well, she thought. If he did, he wouldn't have thrown down such a rhinestone-studded gauntlet. Dance naked to get his attention? Hell's bells, she was a damn sight more creative than that.

THREE HOURS LATER, Chance sat on the rear deck. The platform covering the boat's generator served as a desk for his computer, and he had his phone to his ear. He'd been working ever since they'd finished the dishes. Andi had figured she'd be reasonable and give him some time. After all, he did have a trunkload of awesome obligations. But considering the magnificent surroundings and the delicious isolation, three hours glued to a laptop and cell phone was bordering on excessive.

Time for diversionary action—for his own good, of course.

"Think I'll go for a swim," she said, walking past him.

"Mmm. Have fun." He didn't even look up.

She could have dived right off the side and splashed him, but that was too juvenile. She used the ladder to climb down into the water. She even swam for a little while, to lull him into complacency.

Chance continued to type away on his laptop, the phone clamped between his shoulder and his ear. He could get a permanent neck condition from doing that, she thought.

He needed her to save him from those kinds of compulsive work habits, at least for the next three days. Treading water, she worked her way out of the red suit.

Her aim needed to be perfect for the next part. Too close and she'd soak him, which wasn't her goal. Too far away and it wouldn't have the same effect. She tossed the suit and it landed with a soft plop on the railing about two feet from where he sat.

He glanced up quickly, obviously startled. Then he looked at the suit hanging there, a brilliant statement on the dark blue railing. As she watched him, Andi thought of a bull staring at the matador's red cape. She was hoping for a similar effect.

When he turned his head toward the water, she dived under the surface. When she came up for air, she had to clamp her hand over her mouth to keep from laughing out loud. He was still working on the laptop, but he'd repositioned his chair so he was closer to the railing and had a better view of the water.

A lesser woman might have faked a leg cramp, Andi thought, but she wanted Chance in the water out of desire, not responsibility. He had enough responsibility in his life, as it was.

Thanking her lucky stars that she'd chosen water ballet for her physical-education requirement in college, Andi changed her swimming style from the standard strokes to the more graceful movements she'd learned in the class. Floating on her back and sculling with her hands, she lifted one leg, toes pointed, and slowly allowed herself to sink until at last her toes disappeared under the water.

Breaking the surface, she caught a quick glimpse of Chance before making a dolphin-like forward dive that hid her smile and displayed her bare bottom. He was no longer typing and he'd put down the phone. When she came up again, he was already starting to unfasten his shorts. He was halfway out of them as she began her next move. Arching her back, she propelled herself into a slow backward dive that lifted her breasts above the water, then her hips.

The movement finished with her toes pointing at the sky, her leg muscles firm and…cramping! She gasped and swallowed a mouthful of lake. Oh, God, major cramp. She flailed to the surface, her calf muscle screaming. Her cry for help came out a gurgle. Still thrashing, she looked through a glaze of pain toward the houseboat.

"I'm coming!" Chance shouted, stumbling half-in, half-out of his shorts.

In his panic, his hand shot out toward the generator cover to steady himself and his fist bounced against the laptop, a lightweight piece of technology that skimmed across the fiberglass surface like a hockey puck and flipped over the railing.

Chance made no effort to save it. As the computer landed with a splash and sank beneath the waves, he dived into the lake and started toward her, his powerful stroke cleaving the water with grim purpose.

CHANCE HAD ALWAYS prided himself on his ability to stay calm in a crisis. But when Andi screamed for help, panic grabbed him and shook him until his teeth rattled. Putting the shorts on again would take too long. Desperate to rid himself of them, he became clumsy. Vaguely, he realized he'd knocked the laptop into the water, but he spared it no thought as he tore the seams of his shorts in his frustration, threw them aside and vaulted the railing. Double-checking Andi's position, he dived into the lake and swam harder than he had in his entire life.

He reached her quickly, hooked his arm around her and towed her back to the boat.

"Your laptop," she gasped as they reached the boat and she clung to the ladder.

"I don't give a damn about the laptop." He held on to her as he grasped the other side of the ladder. "What happened?"

"Leg cramp."

"Which one?"

"Left calf."

He managed to hoist her on his knee and reach down with his free hand to massage her leg.

"Chance, never mind me. Get your computer."

"To hell with the computer. You could have drowned out there." His heart beat wildly. He'd never been so scared. Never.

"Because of my own stupidity. That's better, Chance. Go get that laptop, please." She eased her leg out of his grasp.

"You should probably get back in the boat. I'll—"

"No, I think the water's better for it. Will you get that darned thing?"

"Okay. Just stay right here."

"I will. I promise."

Giving her one last glance, he swam to the spot where the laptop had disappeared and dived down. Scooping it off the bottom, he sculled his way to the surface and over to Andi. Using the ladder for support, he lifted the computer, water streaming from every crack, to the deck.

"Oh, Chance!" Andi stared at it, her eyes huge. "Is there any hope?"

"Who cares?"

"I'll...I'll pay to replace it," she said, looking miserable. "But I know that's not the point. You've lost all the stuff you had on there.'' She sniffed. ''I should never have tried to distract you.''

He realized with a shock that not all the moisture on her face was lake water. She was crying. Crying because of what he'd lost. Crying because of a dumb piece of office equipment.

Reaching across the ladder, he closed his hand around her arm. ''Hey,'' he murmured. ''Come here.''

She allowed him to draw her close, but she averted her face. ''I think I'm so smart, so clever. *I'll get him away from that laptop,* I said. Well, I sure managed that, didn't I? What a gal.''

He caught her face and turned it toward him. ''Don't ever apologize for being yourself. I told you to do your damnedest. It was a dare, and I can imagine how you react to dares. And I knocked the stupid thing into the lake, not you.''

Her eyes brimmed with tears that spilled over her wet lashes. ''Because I was teasing you, trying to get you to lose your cool! And then I got a cramp, because I'm not used to pointing my toes like that.''

He smiled tenderly at her. ''It was a good show while it lasted.''

''I was dumb to try it. Now everything's ruined—your spreadsheets, your reports, your list of pros and cons. All gone.''

He was becoming increasingly aware of her naked body cuddled next to him in the water. ''You know what? I don't really give a—'' He paused as he registered what she'd just said. He tilted her face up so he was looking directly into her regret-filled eyes. ''And what list of pros and cons would that be?''

Her eyes widened just like those of a little kid caught climbing on the counter in search of the cookie jar. ''Oh, um, well, I just threw that in. I've heard busy executives often keep—''

"Bull, Andi." He grinned at her. "You were in my files."

"I just wanted to make sure the laptop was working after it fell on the floor."

"You could have determined that without snooping."

She went on the offensive. "And it's a good thing I did! You had that list in a mess."

"I did?"

"A complete mess! What do you mean by referring to my *wacky* view of life?"

Watching emotions blaze in her eyes was an incredibly exhilarating experience. Feeling her slipping and sliding against him in the gentle current was even more exhilarating. "I can't imagine what I was thinking."

"Damn straight. That's why I changed it around."

"You *what?*"

"I rearranged a few things so it's more accurate."

He was nuts about this woman. "You edited my list?"

"It needed some work. Now it looks better." She looked pleased with herself, but then her mouth drooped again. "Or it did. Now it sleeps with the fishes."

He started to laugh. He should have been outraged that she'd messed around with his computer, and furious with himself for dumping it overboard. But the strangest thing had happened. Once he'd accepted that the laptop was unusable, a huge weight had lifted, one he hadn't even known he was carrying. He couldn't work. He physically couldn't work. My God, but he felt liberated.

"Chance," she said, "maybe we should try to dry it out again, like we did after you poured coffee into it. You never know. Miracles do happen."

"Yeah, you're right. Miracles happen all the time. Hang on to the ladder for a minute. I'll get it."

She followed his instructions, moving away from his supporting arm.

When his hand was free, he reached up and took the computer off the deck. Then he held it out over the water...and let go.

Andi shrieked and started after it, but he grabbed her before she could dive under the water.

"What are you doing?" she cried. "There's no way it'll work now!"

"That's right." He pulled her close. "When we're ready to leave, I'll go get it. In the meantime, pucker up those lips and kiss me. We have three hours to make up for."

ANDI COULDN'T BELIEVE the transformation in Chance with the laptop six feet under the surface of the lake. Apparently it had been the anchor weighing him down, reminding him of his obligations. Without it, he seemed reborn. He stripped off his bathing suit and they cavorted in the water like children, chasing and splashing around the cove until they were panting from the exertion.

But beneath the playfulness ran the sensuality that held them both in its passionate grip, and eventually Chance led her back to the boat and made love to her until the sun dipped below the horizon. They called Nicole and found out that she, Bowie and Chandi were flying back to Chicago the next day, which left Andi and Chance free to finish their vacation as they pleased. In celebration, they cooked dinner on the beach, spread out beach towels and made love again.

And it was love they were making. Andi couldn't kid herself that physical pleasure was all she felt when he touched her, when he moved within her. She'd promised Nicole she wouldn't let down her guard, wouldn't let herself get hurt. Maybe if he hadn't knocked his laptop into the lake, she would have managed not to fall so completely in love with him, but this unhampered Chance was impossible to resist.

As they retreated to the boat for the night and Andi snuggled into his arms, she tried not to think of how little time they had left.

HE WOKE HER at dawn with little nibbling kisses. The aroma of coffee drifted from the kitchen, and she turned toward him, thinking she knew what he wanted before his morning coffee.

"Time to get up," he whispered. "Time to fish."

"Fish?"

"It's the very best time. Come on. The coffee's almost done. I have the poles ready."

She reached for him. "I had a very different pole in mind."

He backed away and grinned at her. "Thanks for the compliment. Hey, don't close your eyes again." He leaned down and pried her lids open. "Come out to the rear deck. I set up two chairs. It's more fun with two."

"So's my idea."

"We'll do that later. Now it's time to catch some fish. Fish for breakfast. Yum."

"Doughnuts for breakfast. Yum squared." She swung her legs to the floor. "I remember Bowie saying you loved to fish, but I thought you must have outgrown it."

"Luckily I didn't."

"Luckily." She peered at him. He really did look all excited, as if getting up before the sun was the greatest idea in the world. "Chance, it's barely light out there. Fish don't have alarm clocks. They won't be up yet."

"Fish get up *very* early."

She loved most of the changes in him since he'd dumped the laptop overboard, but she wasn't sure this fishing thing qualified as a positive sign.

"Here, wrap the sleeping bag around you." He draped it over her shoulders. "You're going to love this."

"Oh, yeah." She stumbled down the hall, trailing the sleeping bag like a down-filled bridal train.

He settled her in a deck chair, cast her line for her and put a cup of coffee in her hand. "Isn't this great?"

"Outstanding."

An hour and another pot of coffee later, she turned to him. "So when does the excitement start?"

"Well, they're not biting on the lures we have."

"That's because we should have bought live bait. I told Bowie that we—"

"Your earrings."

"Excuse me?"

"What have we got to lose? Let's try your earrings and see if they go for those."

"You may not have anything to lose, but I have a lovely pair of earrings, a memento from my darling brother-in-law, to lose."

"He can make you another pair. He'd love to. Please, Andi. I really want to catch a fish for breakfast, don't you?"

"You bet," she muttered.

"You don't sound very enthusiastic."

She couldn't bear to squash his excitement, even if she didn't understand it one single bit. "I am. I really am. I'll go get the earrings, one for each of us. Maybe we'll catch two fish!"

"Hey, yeah!"

Turning away, she rolled her eyes and went in search of the earrings.

A half hour later, Andi begged Chance to stop catching fish because they had more than they could eat for breakfast, lunch and dinner.

"You could take some home and freeze them," he said hopefully as they stood on the rear deck with a cooler full of fish.

"Sorry. I have an understanding with my freezer. I don't put dead fish in there and it gives me an endless supply of Fudge Ripple Delight."

"Did you see the way your earrings worked, though?" He held the feathered creation, a little the worse for wear, in one hand. "I've never seen anything like it. Jefferson Sporting Goods needs to get this lure on the market."

Andi looked at him. "Gonna give Bowie a bonus?"

He glanced up, startled. "Yeah, I suppose I should, huh?"

"You know, this may work as a fishing lure, but the idea of earrings isn't bad, either."

"Yeah, if you don't lean too far over the boat while you're wearing them."

Andi laughed. "Hey, cross-promotion! Catch a guy or catch a fish, whichever you're in the mood for."

"I don't know, Andi. Jefferson's always been a pretty conservative company. That sounds kind of goofy, considering our image."

"Too bad you're so restricted. It would be fun to see what would happen if you turned Bowie loose on a campaign for marketing his lure earrings. In fact, if I were you, I'd turn him loose, period. Let him be in charge of new ventures for the company. His creativity is pretty much wasted in sales."

"I'm not sure he has the discipline to carry through if I didn't have him in some structured position."

That did it. "Better erase that old tape, Chance. That's your dad talking, not today's reality. Think about what you've seen on this trip. Think about the night little Chandi was born. When you were sidelined, Bowie picked up the ball without missing a beat."

"It was his wife, his daughter."

"It's his business, too! He's a Jefferson, although he hasn't been given much opportunity to prove it. You have no idea what would happen if you cherished his free spirit instead of scoffing at it, like your dad did all his life."

"I don't scoff."

"Don't you?" She was determined that this time they'd finally get to the end of the argument.

"I get a kick out of Bowie. He's a fun guy."

"Yeah, but fun has its place, right? There's a time for it, and then there's a time to get down to business and be serious."

"Well, of course." He stared at her as if he couldn't believe she'd even bother stating the obvious.

"You don't trust Bowie's ability to get down to business and be serious when the situation demands it. Even though you've had some powerful evidence recently that he's not the fluff-brain you think he is."

He seemed uncomfortable. "I don't know if what happened the other night would translate into business situations."

"The hell it wouldn't! A crisis is a crisis. And in this particular one, you folded. You hate that, don't you? You'd like to forget it, and return to the old days, when you could handle anything and Bowie couldn't be trusted to tie his own shoes without direction."

Chance's gaze grew flinty. "This isn't about me, it's

about him. You haven't lived with him for twenty-seven years. I have. If I gave Bowie the kind of freedom you're talking about, he'd be all over the map. He'd flit from one thing to another, never settling on anything long enough to make a success of it."

"Well, I'm no different. Does that make us so bad?"

He didn't say anything, but the answer was there in his eyes.

She'd guessed that was his opinion of her. She just hadn't wanted to think about it. "Bowie and I are fun to have around once in a while, but don't count on us for the long haul, because we don't have that kind of stamina, right?"

He took her by both arms. "Let's take Bowie out of this for a minute. You have tremendous potential, Andi. I'm not so blinded by lust that I can't see how capable you are. When you were working with Bowie on yoga, I realized that you're a natural teacher. If you'd just grab hold of something, maybe open your own yoga school, for example, you could be—"

"Like you?" Had he not made this comment, she would have taken great satisfaction in having him learn from Nicole that she'd gone into business for herself. Now he'd suppose it was his idea, not hers, which took the incentive right out of it. "You want me to drive myself day and night to achieve some goal someone else set for me? No, thanks."

He released her and turned away. "I suppose you think I should just abandon Jefferson Sporting Goods to Bowie and run away with you to some desert isle where we can live on love."

Tears of frustration filled her eyes, but she blinked them back. "Bring Bowie's fishing lure and you have a deal."

He bowed his head. "I can't, Andi."

Her throat hurt from the effort not to cry. She'd set herself up for this, after all. "Can't or won't?"

He turned, his eyes filled with agony. "Won't, then. Good or bad, I'm the way life has made me. I can't imagine turning the company over to Bowie, no matter what I've seen on this trip. And I can't image life without the challenge and the competition I'm used to. I'd go crazy on a desert island."

"And all that you love about your life would drive me crazy."

He swallowed. "I've been asking myself if there was any way you could come to Chicago, any way we could work out some arrangement."

She closed her eyes against the pain and took a long, shaky breath before she dared speak. "What we've found here is too fragile, Chance." She forced herself to look at him while she finished. "We'd kill that special feeling in a week."

He gazed at her in silence. Finally he spoke, his voice husky. "Please tell me we didn't just kill it this morning."

If the ache in her heart was any indication, she still loved him, stubborn type-A behavior and all, with a fierceness that promised to give her a great deal of misery in the future. "Is your laptop still in the lake?"

"Unless you hooked it with one of your wild casts."

"Would you expect me to cast any other way?"

"No."

She held out her arms and gave a seductive little shimmy. "Then let the good times roll."

14

CHANCE MARVELED at Andi's generosity of spirit as she threw herself into their last full day as if there were no tomorrow. He'd never encountered that kind of resilience and he was both awestruck and fascinated.

In the morning she made love to him with gusto, and in the afternoon she taught him water ballet until she nearly drowned herself laughing as he gracefully pointed his toes in the air. Most women he'd known would have spent hours in hurt silence after a conversation like the one he'd had with Andi on the rear deck of the boat. But as the sun set behind the cliffs, ushering in their last night together, Andi was standing on the beach, instructing him on the finer points of the macarena.

The only problem was, he couldn't imagine who he'd be dancing with once Andi was no longer a part of his life. But they'd come to an impasse. She apparently expected him to become some sort of beach bum, which was out of the question. As for transplanting her to Chicago, he'd pretty much given up that idea. She was probably right—their carefree relationship wouldn't survive once he returned to the world of big-city business.

"You have a decent sense of rhythm, Jefferson," she said, bobbing in time with him as they undulated through the moves of the dance, she in her black swimsuit and he in his bathing trunks.

"You should have seen my rendition of the hokey-pokey in kindergarten. I put them all in the shade."

"I'll bet. You know what this dance would be good for?"

He kept up the rhythm. "Yeah. Slapping mosquitoes. Just got one."

"I was thinking of people who work at computers all day. See how I'm moving my arms around?"

"I love watching you move your arms around. I love watching you move your everything around."

"But think of it. If you called a macarena break every hour or so, they might not get that thing they get, you know—carpal tunnel syndrome."

"Or how about a yoga break?" He stopped dancing and gazed at her.

"Well, I suppose." Her glance was wary.

Despite what he'd vowed to himself, the idea was too good to ignore. "Come to Chicago, Andi. There are carpal tunnel sufferers in every office on Michigan Avenue. With your talent and charisma, you could build up a business in no time."

She closed the distance between them and took his face in her hands. "And you? What would you be doing while I ran up and down Michigan Avenue in my tights and leotard?"

"Carrying your yoga mat."

"Never kid a kidder, Chance." She stood on tiptoe and kissed him gently. "You'd be working those fourteen-hour days Nicole's told me about. I'd be lucky to catch a glimpse of the tailored sleeve of your Armani suit jacket as you whipped by."

He wound his arms around her and almost groaned aloud at the pleasure of pulling her close. "Wrong. I'd go without sleep before I gave up making love to you."

"Did you hear what you just said?" she admonished, and kissed him again, slipping her tongue into his mouth before drawing away again.

"Yeah, I asked you to keep French-kissing me for about a hundred years, give or take a decade."

"You offered to give up sleep. Not work. Sleep. No, my workaholic lover. I'm not adding myself to your packed schedule."

"Then I'll just have to kidnap you." He delved into her lush mouth and tried to forget that tomorrow at this time he wouldn't be able to kiss her. He wouldn't be able to run his hand over her smooth back and cup her firm behind. He wouldn't be able to pull down the straps of her swimsuit and kiss her warm breasts.

And he wouldn't have to try to remember where he'd thrown the box of condoms when he'd brought them down to the beach. During these last few hours, he'd considered stringing the box around his neck so he'd never be without, just in case she started doing what she was doing right this minute. She'd reached inside his swimsuit to caress him in ways that meant he'd better find that box, and fast.

"Wait," he said, gasping as she fondled him with the exquisite talent he'd learned to associate with Andi. "Let me get the—" He glanced toward the towel where he remembered leaving the box of condoms. A raven was pecking at the box. "Hey! Scram!"

He ran, or more accurately, considering his aroused state, he lurched toward the towel. The raven took the box in its beak and flapped skyward. "Oh, no, you don't, bird-brain!" He leaped like a star pass receiver and grabbed the box, wrenching it from the bird's claws. Then he did a belly flop into the sand. It knocked the wind from him, but it wasn't hitting his belly that caused him to grimace in pain.

"Chance?" She hurried over to him and crouched beside him. "Are you okay?"

"I think...I broke...my...pride and joy."

"Turn over and let me look."

He spit out some sand and struggled to draw a breath. "You're laughing, aren't you?"

There was a muffled sound, and then she cleared her throat. "I wouldn't laugh about a thing like this. Come on, roll over."

He did, drawing another tortured breath in the process.

"Poor baby." She brushed the sand from his heaving chest. "Knocked the breath right out of you."

"Damn wildlife."

"Let's see if I can inflate you again." She eased his swimsuit down. "Why lookee here! It's a valve!"

Laughing made his chest hurt, but he couldn't help it. "I think I squashed it."

"Oh, I'll bet it still works."

Darned if she wasn't right. Not long after she put her mouth there, he felt ready to explode. "Easy, Andi. Easy, sweetheart."

She kissed her way up his chest and smiled down at him. "Time to put the cap on," she said, taking the condom box from his unresisting fingers. She pulled out a cellophane-wrapped package. "Uh-oh. Beak holes."

Chance groaned. "I don't want to hear this. If that featherbrain ruined all of them..."

"Uh-oh. More beak holes."

Chance struggled to a sitting position. "Let's see."

"I have a better idea." She grabbed the box and raced down to the water. "We'll test them and find out if they leak."

He eased his trunks over his erection and slowly got up to follow her. As he started toward the lake, he cursed the bird kingdom in general and ravens in particular. "Andi, I don't know if—" Whap! A water-filled condom hit him in the face. "Hey!"

"It had a leak, but I hated to waste such a perfect water balloon," she said, laughing.

"Water balloons," he mumbled, heading toward her again. Bam! Another bulging condom hit him on the chin.

"Another leaker," she called out gaily.

He was dripping. "I'm trying to make love to one of the Marx Brothers," he muttered to himself. Another water-swollen condom sailed toward him, but he ducked and caught it. It didn't break. Good. He needed some ammunition.

"Leak city," she sang out, busy with her experiment at the edge of the water.

"I'm beginning to think you don't want that valve job, after all," he said, approaching her. He held the filled condom behind his back.

"I do." She glanced up at him, her expression impish. "I just don't want any surprises, if you know what I mean."

He dropped to his knees in the shallow water and grabbed her. "Too bad." He broke the water-filled condom over her head, soaking her hair.

She shrieked and struggled in his grip as water dripped down her face. "No fair!"

"You're a fine one to talk. Now kiss me, and make it quick."

She stopped struggling and turned her face up to his, her expression seductive.

"That's better." He started to kiss her just as a condom of water broke over his head. "Ah!" He lifted his head and shook the water from his eyes as she giggled. "Okay, that does it." He scooped her up.

"Wait!" She struggled and kicked. "Put me down! No fair using superior strength."

"If you can be sneaky, I can be macho." He waded out until the water licked his thighs. Then he dropped her with a splash. "Whoops."

She floundered around and finally staggered upright, sputtering, her hair streaming in her eyes. Then she pushed him. He was laughing so hard he couldn't keep his balance, and he went under.

As he came up, he grabbed her and tugged her in with him as she squirmed and flailed in his arms. "Were any of those damn things any good?"

"One!" she said, gasping and trying to get away from him.

"Where is it?"

"In my—oh, no, there it goes!"

"Where?"

"I tucked it in the front of my suit. It's floating away!"

"Where?" Chance lunged through the dancing, star-flecked water. Several times he imagined he saw the floating condom, but nothing was there.

"It's over there!" Andi pointed to her left.

"I don't see it. Oh, God, where did it go?"

"Here. I found it."

"Where is it?"

She stuck out her tongue. The condom was on it. And he was pretty sure it had never floated away in the first place.

"Oh, you're asking for it." He advanced on her.

She pulled the condom off her tongue and backed up, grinning all the while. "Just a little joke."

"Uh-huh. And now it's my turn."

She chuckled as she continued to back toward shore. "You should have seen yourself looking for it."

"I'm sure I was a riot." He stalked her patiently as his blood heated.

"Actually, there's more than one."

"Now *that's* hilarious. I was killing myself and it wasn't even the last one."

"I left a couple in the box."

"I'm only interested in the one in your hand."

"This one?" Smiling, she held it up.

"That one." He launched himself at her and grabbed the condom as they both tumbled down in the shallow water. He was on her in a second, peeling her suit off as she squirmed in the wet sand. She was no match for him, and he soon tossed the suit up on the beach.

"Chance!" she said, panting, "I'll get sand in my hair!"

Holding her with his upper body, he wrenched away his suit and snapped the condom on. "When this is over, I'll wash it for you, strand by strand. But by God, we're doing this right here, right now." And as the water lapped at their bodies, he buried himself in her.

This could be the last time. The sudden thought pierced the red haze of his passion. Everything in him rebelled at the idea of never loving her again.

"I need you, Andi," he murmured into her ear.

"You have me."

"When you come to visit Nicole—"

"No. I won't spoil this with scattered, stolen moments."

"Andi." Her name had become a plea.

"Make love with me, Chance." She began to rock gently against him. "Because I need you, too."

15

FOR THE FIRST FEW DAYS after Andi said goodbye to Chance at the airport, she invited friends to the movies until her friends grew weary of the routine and she'd seen every comedy playing at least twice. If a comedian was booked on The Strip, she was there, no matter the cost of the ticket. Then she recorded all the "I Love Lucy" episodes she could find in the television guide so she'd have something to watch when she couldn't sleep.

Sometimes her raucous laughter threatened to turn into tears, and then she'd put on loud rock music until the feeling passed or the neighbors pounded on the walls of her apartment. She beat back her tears with Dave Barry columns, "Beavis and Butthead" and David Letterman.

By God, Chance would not make her cry.

She talked to Nicole often and downplayed the significance of the time she'd spent alone with Chance. Nicole said she'd barely seen Chance since he'd come back. He seemed to have lost himself in his work. So he wasn't pining away for her, Andi thought. But the satisfaction of knowing she'd made the right decision didn't help as much as she'd hoped it would.

Andi's parents spent two weeks in Chicago soon after Nicole and the baby arrived home, so Andi decided to save her week with Nicole for Chandi's first Christmas. Besides, the longer she put off seeing Chance at some family function, the better.

As the weeks went by, she realized there weren't

enough comedies in the world to keep her mind off Chance. His idea of arranging yoga classes for computer operators in large businesses rustled around in her head until, desperate for the distraction, she finally called a couple of Las Vegas's bigger corporations. The response was encouraging. Before she quite realized what was happening, she'd set up a schedule that kept her going five days a week and caused her to cancel the small classes she had been teaching for a local yoga school. She was forced to print up her own business cards. The irony of it didn't escape her.

She was so busy, in fact, that she rarely stayed home. Looking forward to a quiet Friday night for the first time in weeks, she'd even decided against stopping by the video store on her way home, which had been her recent pattern whenever she anticipated being alone for the weekend.

Juggling her mail from the box in the hall downstairs and an order of Chinese takeout, she opened the door and promptly threw everything up in the air. Fried rice, almond chicken and advertising circulars rained down as she stared in disbelief at the man sitting in her living room, a duffel bag beside him on the couch.

Chance stood and came toward her. He was dressed casually in a T-shirt and jeans. Weekend wear.

He glanced at the food scattered over the carpet. "It's not exactly fudge sauce, but I guess we can work with it."

She backed away from him. "Oh, no, you don't! You're not showing up now. I didn't even have to rent videos tonight! I suppose that means nothing to you, but—"

"You're right, it means absolutely nothing to me." He stared blankly at her. "What videos?"

"Never mind. The point is, they're not here."

"Good." He came closer. "I don't want to watch videos, anyway."

"I know what you want to do, and we're not doing it." Her heart was pounding so loud she could barely hear herself speak. "No, sir. I'm aware that Las Vegas is an airline hub."

"Andi, this is a strange conversation."

"It makes perfect sense to me! You may think you can drop by whenever you're in the neighborhood and stop over for a quickie, but that's not how it works, Mister Sex-on-Your-Mind. I may be easy, but I'm not consistently easy."

He grinned. "Couldn't prove it by me. Your apartment key is floating all over the place." He dangled a key he pulled from his pocket.

Oh, that smile. It melted something she'd been trying to freeze for weeks. But she was fighting for her sanity, and she took a deep breath and plunged on. "That's another thing! What do you mean, barging in here uninvited...what do you mean, my key's floating everywhere?"

"A few weeks ago, I went to see Bowie and Nicole when your folks were in town, and I asked if anybody could loan me a key to your apartment. They all had keys."

"Well, of course they did. They're family." She held out her hand. "But you don't get one. Give it here."

"I'm family."

"Only in a very general way."

He took her hand and placed a kiss on her palm. "I'm here to make it more specific."

She jerked her hand away. That touch set her on fire. She couldn't allow it. "I'll just bet. The key, Jefferson. You are not invited for the weekend, if that's what you had in mind. I see you even brought luggage. I made our terms very clear and you're violating our agreement.''

He seemed to be having a hard time keeping a straight face. ''I want to negotiate new terms.''

''I should have known. You probably want another little valve job, right? Sorry, but the warranty has expired. You men are so predictable.''

''Okay, let's start with this. I love you.''

She rolled her eyes. ''Oh, yeah, like nobody's ever tried *that* line to get what they want from their little hotsie-totsie.''

''Then let's try this, Miss Hotsie-Totsie. Will you marry me?''

''I suppose next you'll—'' She stared at him. ''What did you say?''

''Marry me, Andi. Please. I'm going out of my mind.''

All the fight went out of her. ''Oh, Chance. You don't know what you're asking.''

''I think I do. I'm reasonably bright—I took phonics in school, and the sentence only has four words in it. Will…you…marry…me?''

She gazed at him as she struggled with her answer. She'd missed him horribly in the past few weeks. How she longed to fling herself into his arms and agree to anything he wanted. But what would they do to each other, living under the pressure of his frantic life? She'd go into the marriage knowing she wanted to change him, and that wasn't fair.

Taking a deep breath, she looked him right in the eye. ''No.''

''Why not?''

''Because I love you.''

''Well, now we're getting somewhere.'' He closed the distance between them, fried rice mashing under the soles of his running shoes, and pulled her into his arms.

"Chance, don't." She tried to push him away, but not very hard. A girl had only so much willpower. "Getting physically involved again will only make us more miserable, in the long run."

"Not if we get married." He ducked his head and tried to kiss her.

She twisted away. "I just told you—"

"That you won't marry me because you love me." He captured her chin and made her look at him. "Have I got that straight?"

She was drowning in his blue, blue eyes. "I know it sounds backward, but it's true."

"It sounds fine to me. I'm becoming an expert in Andi-think. All I had to know was that you love me. The rest is details."

"The rest is the whole point!"

"No." He combed his fingers through her hair and cradled her head in his hand. "I used to think so, too. I thought the obstacle was my job, but finally it occurred to me that the only real obstacle was whether or not you loved me—whether I was the kind of guy who could coax you into giving up your freedom."

"Of course you are, but *you* aren't free, Chance."

He smiled. "Oh, yes, I am."

She looked into his eyes and saw something she'd never seen there before—a gleam of sheer exuberance. "Okay, what have you done?"

"Taken back my life. Come share it with me."

"You quit?" Her pulse raced. "Because of me?"

"No. I had to do this for myself. I might have come here tonight and discovered you didn't love me, after all. Those days on the houseboat might have been just a fling for you."

"Oh, no." A joyous song was wending its way through her heart, building in volume the longer she gazed into his eyes. She'd probably still have to live in the big-city atmosphere of Chicago, but that was a small compromise. "It was never just a fling. You have no idea how miserable I've been since you left."

He sighed. "Good."

"Good?" She pushed at his chest. "That's not nice, hoping I've been miserable. I was hoping you were doing just fine."

"Liar." He glanced down at the spot where she'd pushed him, released her and walked back to the duffel bag sitting on the couch.

"Chance?" Oh, God, she'd offended him. "I didn't really mean to shove you away. I was kidding. You know me. Always joking around."

"Don't worry." He shot her a rakish smile. "You won't get rid of me that easy." He zipped open his duffel and pulled out another T-shirt. "When you pushed at my chest, I suddenly remembered your present." He tossed the shirt at her. "It may not look like much now, but once you put it on and wet it down, I'm sure it'll be outstanding."

She held up the T-shirt and realized it was identical to his. She'd been too preoccupied to pay attention to what was printed on the front. Now she looked more closely, and glanced up at him. *"Bowie and Chance's Bait and Tackle?"*

He looked so proud of himself he almost preened. "Yeah. We're partners. It was his idea to try this, and after all that you said finally sunk into my stubborn brain, I realized his solution was brilliant."

"Is it connected to Jefferson Sporting Goods?"

"Nope. Mom may insist we get a discount on merchandise, but it's an independent operation."

"Your mother?" Andi felt as if her brain was shorting out from the overload of information.

"She's running Jefferson Sporting Goods now. Remember when I said nobody would handle things if I didn't, and you warned me not to be so sure?"

"I remember."

"Well, when Bowie and I left for a week, she started dropping by the office, just to check on things. Turns out she loves the business and always had a secret desire to be in charge. I never knew. She's learning all the ropes and becoming really great at it."

"Amazing."

"So." He focused on her, his gaze like a laser. "Do you really like the shirt?"

"I really do."

"Do you like it a lot?" he prompted.

"Well, sure." She held it out in front of her. "The crossed fishing poles make a good logo, and you have Bowie's name first, which was generous." She studied the shirt, looking for more things to praise. That was when she saw the small lettering beneath the logo. *Lake Mead, Nevada.* Her glance came up to lock with his, and she couldn't keep the grin from her face. "Here?"

"It's where Bowie's lure works." He crossed the room. "And if you'd been stubborn about marrying me, I'd planned to move in next door and lay siege."

"Oh, Chance!" She flung herself into his arms. "You can start anytime."

He caught her and held on tight. "Start what?"

"Laying siege."

"But you've already said yes."

She gave him a hot, wet and very suggestive kiss. "No, I haven't. I just admitted to loving you. You're gonna have to work to win my hand, Chance Jefferson. You're gonna have to lay seige, just like you said. And I can hardly wait."

HARLEQUIN®

Temptation.

Move over, St. Nick!

Jo Cassidy had always had a weakness for cowboys.
And rugged Russ Gibson definitely made her weak.
But Jo was looking for commitment. And for that she
needed someone more reliable, more solid...less sexy.
That is, until Russ convinced her that all she
wanted for Christmas was him!

If you love Vicki Lewis Thompson,
don't miss her next title:

661 SANTA IN A STETSON
from Harlequin Temptation®

Available in December 1997
wherever Harlequin books are sold.

Born in the USA

Every month there's another title from one
of your favorite authors!

October 1997
Romeo in the Rain by Kasey Michaels
When Courtney Blackmun's daughter brought home Mr. Tall,
Dark and Handsome, Courtney wanted to send the young
matchmaker to her room! Of course, that meant the single
New Jersey mom would be left alone with the irresistibly
attractive Adam Richardson....

November 1997
Intrusive Man by Lass Small
Indiana's Hannah Calhoun had enough on her hands taking
care of her young son, and the last thing she needed was a
man complicating things—especially Max Simmons, the
gorgeous cop who had eased himself right into her little boy's
heart...and was making his way into hers.

December 1997
Crazy Like a Fox by Anne Stuart
Moving in with her deceased husband's—*eccentric*—family
in Louisiana meant a whole new life for Margaret Jaffrey and
her nine-year-old daughter. But the beautiful young widow
soon finds herself seduced by the slower pace and the much-
too-attractive cousin-in-law, Peter Andrew Jaffrey....

**BORN IN THE USA: Love, marriage—
and the pursuit of family!**

Available at your favorite retail outlet!

Look us up on-line at: http://www.romance.net   BUSA3

CHRISTMAS MIRACLES

really can happen, and Christmas
dreams can come true!

BETTY NEELS,
Carole Mortimer and Rebecca Winters

bring you the magic of Christmas in this wonderful
holiday collection of romantic stories intertwined
with Christmas dreams come true.

Join three of your favorite romance authors as they
celebrate the festive season in their own special style!

Available in November at your favorite retail store.

HARLEQUIN®

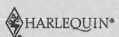 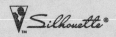

Indiscreet

Camilla Ferrand wants everyone, especially her dying grandfather, to stop worrying about her. So she tells them that she is engaged to be married. But with no future husband in sight, it's going to be difficult to keep up the pretense. Then she meets the very handsome and mysterious Benedict Ellsworth who generously offers to accompany Camilla to her family's estate—as her most devoted fiancé.

But at what cost does this *generosity* come?

From the bestselling author of *Impulse*

CANDACE CAMP

Available in November 1997
at your favorite retail outlet.

*Candace Camp also writes for Silhouette® as Kristen James